# DOCTOR WHO
# REVENGE OF THE CYBERMEN

# DOCTOR WHO
# REVENGE OF THE CYBERMEN

Based on the BBC television serial by
Gerry Davis by arrangement with the British
Broadcasting Corporation

## TERRANCE DICKS

**TARGET**

A TARGET BOOK
*published by*
the Paperback Division of
W.H. ALLEN & CO. plc

A Target Book
Published in 1976
by the Paperback Division of
W.H. Allen & Co plc
338 Ladbroke Grove, London W10 5AH
Reprinted 1979, 1981, 1983 and 1991.

The BBC producer of *Revenge of the Cybermen* was Barry Letts
the director was Michael E. Briant

The role of the Doctor was played by Tom Baker

Printed and bound in Great Britain by
Cox & Wyman Ltd, Reading, Berkshire

ISBN 0 426 10997 X

# Contents

# The Creation of the Cybermen

Centuries ago by our Earth time, a race of men on the far-distant planet of Telos sought immortality. They perfected the art of cybernetics—the reproduction of machine functions in human beings. As bodies became old and diseased, they were replaced limb by limb, with plastic and steel.

Finally, even the human circulation and nervous system were recreated, and brains replaced by computers. The first cybermen were born.

Their metal limbs gave them the strength of ten men, and their in-built respiratory system allowed them to live in the airless vacuum of space. They were immune to cold and heat, and immensely intelligent and resourceful. Their large, silver bodies became practically indestructible.

Their main impediment was one that only flesh and blood men would have recognized: they had no heart, no emotions, no feelings. They lived by the inexorable laws of pure logic. Love, hate, anger, even fear, were eliminated from their lives when the last flesh was replaced by plastic.

They achieved their immortality at a terrible price. They became dehumanised monsters. And, like human monsters down through all the ages of Earth, they became aware of the lack of love and feeling in their lives and substituted another goal—power!

# 1

# Return to Peril

In the silent blackness of deep space, the gleaming metal shape of Space Beacon Nerva hung like a giant gyroscope. There was no indication of life—it looked silent, somehow dead. Inside the huge space station too, all seemed silent and empty. Control-rooms, corridors, living quarters, everywhere was deserted.

In an empty control-room, the air seemed to shimmer and blur. Three people appeared out of nowhere; a slim, dark, pretty girl, a broad-shouldered, square-jawed young man and a very tall, thin man whose motley collection of vaguely Bohemian garments included an incredibly long scarf, and a battered soft hat jammed on top of a mop of wildly-curling brown hair. The girl was called Sarah Jane Smith, the young man Harry Sullivan. Both were companions of the third arrival, that mysterious traveller in Time and Space known only as 'The Doctor'.

Sarah shivered and looked round, glad to recognise familiar surroundings. 'Thank Heavens for that, we've made it.' But something seemed to puzzle her. The place was the same yet subtly different. She looked hopefully at the Doctor. 'We have made it—haven't we?'

The Doctor could never understand that Sarah sometimes found it hard to share his habitual cheery optimism. 'Of course we've made it, Sarah. Did you think we wouldn't?'

Sarah nodded decisively. 'In these past few weeks, yes. Quite frequently.'

Harry Sullivan grinned, thinking to himself that Sarah had excellent reasons for her recent doubts. He'd doubted his own chance of survival quite a few times since first meeting the Doctor.

It had all started with that terrifying business of the Giant Robot.* Harry Sullivan, newly appointed medical officer to the United Nations Intelligence Taskforce—UNIT for short—had been given the job of looking after that organisation's Scientific Adviser, who was in fact the Doctor, recently recovered from some mysterious illness which had left him, it appeared, a changed man. The Robot business had been bad enough, but at least it had all happened on Earth—an Earth which Harry sometimes wondered if he'd ever see again. Rashly following the Doctor and Sarah into what looked like an old-fashioned Police Box, Harry had found himself whipped away from Earth and thrown into a series of horrifying adventures in Time and Space.

They had just escaped, barely, from the most recent, an attempt by the Doctor to go back in Time and prevent the growing menace of the Daleks.† On this occasion they had travelled not in the Police Box, the Doctor's TARDIS, but by means of a Time Bracelet provided by the Doctor's mysterious superiors, the Time Lords. Now that same bracelet had brought them back to the space station, scene of an earlier adventure, where they were supposed to pick up the TARDIS and go home. Harry looked round the empty

* See 'Doctor Who and the Giant Robot'.
† See 'Doctor Who and the Genesis of the Daleks'.

8

control-room. 'I say, Doctor, the TARDIS isn't here.'

The Doctor sighed. 'I was wondering when you'd notice that.'

Sarah stared at him accusingly. 'Something's gone wrong, hasn't it?'

The Doctor held up his wrist, adorned with a heavy, elaborately-decorated bracelet. 'There's really nothing that *can* go wrong with a Time Bracelet ...' He shook the bracelet, holding it close to his ear. 'Apart from a molecular short-circuit,' he added sadly.

'All right, Doctor,' said Sarah. 'Tell us the worst. Where *is* the TARDIS?'

The Doctor rubbed his fingers through his tangled curls. 'Well,' he began hopefully, 'I think there's been a little temporal displacement, you see. We've arrived too early and the TARDIS just hasn't got here yet.' The Doctor beamed, as if this solved everything.

Sarah wasn't satisfied. 'How early are we?'

'Oh, about a thousand years or so.' The Doctor looked carefully at the equipment in the control-room. 'In this era, the space station's doing the kind of job it was originally meant for—a beacon to guide and service space freighters.'

'So we've got to hang about here for a thousand years or so, waiting for the TARDIS to turn up?'

'No, of course not, Sarah. The TARDIS will be drifting towards us through Time—and as soon as the Time Lords realise what's happened, they'll hurry it up for us.' The Doctor slipped the Time Bracelet from his wrist, shook it again and tossed it casually on to a nearby control console.

Harry looked at him in astonishment. 'Don't you want it any more?'

'No. It's no more use to us now.'

'Can I have it then—as a souvenir?'

The Doctor chuckled. 'Certainly, Harry. But you'd better look after it very carefully.'

'Oh, I shall. Thanks awfully!' Harry reached eagerly for the Time Bracelet—just as it shimmered and vanished. He turned indignantly to the Doctor. 'You *knew* that was going to happen!'

'Who, me?' asked the Doctor innocently. Before Harry could protest further, the Doctor went on, 'Let's take a look around to pass the time, shall we? Now as I remember, this door leads to the perimeter corridor ...' The Doctor slid open the connecting door. A stiff corpse fell out, landing almost on top of him.

Instinctively the Doctor jumped back, and the falling body crashed to the floor. All three stared horrified at the corpse for a moment. It was the body of a man in his thirties, wearing the simple coverall-type uniform of a Space Technician. Harry knelt by the body and made a swift examination. 'He's dead all right, poor chap. Dead some time ...'

'How long?' snapped the Doctor.

Harry shrugged. 'Hard to say. A week or two, could be longer. There's very little putrefaction, though.'

The Doctor nodded. 'Sterile environment, you see. Cause of death?'

'No sign of injury ... I'd have to do a proper autopsy.'

Sarah recovered from her horror-stricken silence. 'He must have been leaning against the other side of that door when he died. But they wouldn't have just left him there, not for two weeks, would they, Doctor?'

'Not unless there was something very badly wrong

here.' The Doctor stepped past the body and went through the door. Then he stopped, as if frozen in horror. Harry and Sarah came up behind, looking past him into the corridor. They too stopped, frozen in the same horrified disbelief.

The long perimeter corridor stretched ahead, curving out of sight in the distance as it followed the outer contours of the space station. The corridor was full of dead bodies. Corpse after corpse, a long line of them stretching ahead, twisted and contorted in the stiff, ungainly attitudes of sudden death. Sarah buried her face in the Doctor's shoulder. 'They're all dead. Everyone on this space station must be dead . . .'

But Sarah was wrong. Not everyone on Nerva Beacon was dead. Not yet. In a small control-room on the far side of the base, a Communications Technician named Warner was slumped over his control panel, face grey with fatigue. He jerked into life as a sharp pinging signal-sound filled the room. Rubbing his eyes, he checked his space-radar screen, and flipped a switch. 'This is Nerva Beacon calling Pluto–Earth flight one-five. Are you reading me?'

A voice crackled out of the speaker. 'We read you clear, Nerva Beacon. Our dropover time estimated at thirteen-twenty.'

'Your dropover is cancelled, repeat, cancelled. This beacon is now a quarantined zone, due to an outbreak of space-plague. Your dropover is transferred to Ganymede Beacon, one-nine-six-zero-seven-zero-two. Shall I repeat?'

'Thank you, Nerva Beacon, we have co-ordinates.'

There was a moment's pause, then the voice from the speaker said awkwardly, 'How bad is it? If there's anything we can do ...'

Warner grinned wryly, and tried to force some cheerfulness into his voice. 'Thanks for the offer, but our medical team is getting things under control.'

There was another pause and then the voice said, 'We have a query, Nerva Beacon. Our First Officer has a brother doing a tour with you—Crewmaster Colville. He'd like to know if he's O.K., or ...'

Warner gave a wince of pain, but he carefully kept his voice matter-of-fact. 'Hold contact, I'll check for you.' He flipped his internal communications switch, closing the space relay so the pilot couldn't hear him. 'Commander Stevenson ...'

In a nearby crewroom, Commander Stevenson rolled wearily from his bunk as he heard his name. He stumbled to the control console. 'Stevenson here.'

Warner's voice came over the intercom. 'I'm in contact with the Pluto–Earth flight, sir. One of the crew wants news of his brother, Crewmaster Colville. What do I tell him?'

Stevenson rubbed a hand across his aching red-rimmed eyes. Colville was dead of course. Everyone was dead except for Warner, Stevenson himself and the two other men in the room with him. Four survivors, from a crew of over forty. Grimly Stevenson said, 'Tell him Colville's fine, and the epidemic's almost over. Just that and nothing else.' He switched off the intercom and stood leaning wearily against the console for a moment. One of the men on the bunks, a civilian named Kellman, propped himself up on an elbow. Since he had no duties, nothing to do but eat and sleep, he looked plump and rested, unlike the grey-haired Stevenson, whose face was drawn with exhaustion.

With his habitual sneer Kellman said, 'Why don't you tell them the truth, Commander?'

Stevenson was too tired even to be angry. 'I am following the orders of Earth Central Control.'

'Operating the Beacon to the last man?'

'If necessary, yes.' There was a tinge of contempt in Stevenson's voice. 'You're a civilian, *Professor* Kellman. You wouldn't understand.'

Kellman yawned and stretched luxuriously. 'How much longer can you go on—three of you trying to do the work of forty-three?'

The third man in the room was awake by now, a tough, burly crew-member called Lester, fiercely loyal to his Commander. He got slowly off his bunk and moved menacingly towards Kellman.

'Don't worry, Professor. We've managed for two weeks, we'll manage for another one.'

'And another—and another? This Beacon's finished, Lester . . .'

Stevenson spoke with weary patience, 'Nerva Beacon *has* to remain operative until every space-freighter has the new asteroid on its star-chart. Until then, there's a constant danger of space collision . . .'

Rudely Kellman interrupted, 'You deserve a medal, all of you. Self-sacrifice beyond the call of stupidity . . .'

Lester moved quickly towards him, a brawny clenched fist drawn back, but Kellman, fresh and alert after plenty of sleep, dodged quickly past the exhausted crewman and slipped out of the room, closing the door behind him. Lester slumped back on to his bunk.

Stevenson gave a sympathetic grin. 'I know. I've lost most of my crew these last few weeks, good friends among them. Yet a miserable creature like that is still alive.'

Lester stretched out. 'Shut himself away in his office, didn't he, sir, soon as the plague started. Now it seems to be over, he's poking his nose out of his rathole.' Lester's voice slurred, his head nodded and he drifted back into sleep.

Stevenson went to his desk and started shuffling through his duty-rosters. Three men to do the work of forty. Kellman was right—it was ridiculous. It was only possible because all three worked to a killing schedule; long hours of duty with the bare minimum of sleep. Kellman had refused to even attempt to help, claiming that he lacked the necessary skills. This despite the fact that he was a trained exographer, a planetary surveyor sent to investigate the new asteroid that had so mysteriously appeared in the orbit of Jupiter. But Kellman's job had been finished before the space-plague struck. Now he was just a useless passenger, an irritant to the nerves of the other survivors. Wondering why the space plague had seen fit to spare someone who was not only unnecessary but nasty with it, Stevenson carried on with his impossible task.

For the rest of her life Sarah Jane Smith was to be haunted by the memory of that nightmarish stumble down the long curved corridor filled with corpses. She closed her eyes for most of it, clutching the Doctor's sleeve and trying not to think about the stiff, pathetic figures as she edged blindly past them. Once a corpse, disturbed by the Doctor's passing, fell suddenly towards her with claw-like hands that seemed to be reaching out. Sarah choked off her scream and moved grimly on.

Suddenly she became aware that the Doctor had stopped. She opened her eyes. A steel door stretched across the corridor, barring the way ahead of them. The Doctor operated the control panel set in the corridor wall. Nothing happened. 'Seems to be jammed,' he muttered. 'The controls are locked.'

Harry looked grim. 'So we can't get any further?' He glanced quickly at Sarah, wondering if she would be able to bear it if they had to retrace their steps.

The Doctor nodded towards the line of bodies stretching away behind them. 'These poor chaps couldn't get any further, either,' he said thoughtfully. 'They were sealed off in this aft-section, left here to die. So whatever did it must be on the other side of this door.' He produced his sonic-screwdriver and began to dismantle the door control panel.

Harry said dubiously, 'Are you sure you want that door open, Doctor?'

The Doctor nodded. 'It's always better to know what you're up against, Harry. Besides, if the co-ordinates slip, the TARDIS could pop up almost anywhere on this Beacon. We've got to be able to move around and find it ...'

The Doctor went on working. Harry gave Sarah a consoling hug. 'Don't worry, old girl, we'll soon be out of here.' Sarah managed a rather feeble smile.

As they watched the Doctor plunge into a tangle of electronic circuitry with his usual cheerful confidence, something moved along the corridor behind them.

It scurried between the corpses, triangular in shape, metallic body scaled like a silver-fish, large red electronic eyes glowing on top of its head. It was like a giant metal rat. As Sarah and Harry watched the Doctor work, the strange metal beast slid closer and closer to them. When it was just a few feet from Sarah's back, it stopped, as if poised to spring ...

## 2

## The Cybermat Strikes

Sarah's life was saved by her exceptionally good peripheral vision. The metal creature moved a little to one side of her, as if to get a clear spring at her throat. Sarah caught a flash of movement in the corner of her eye, spun round and reacted in true feminine style; she let out a loud, hearty scream. The Doctor whirled round, and the sonic-screwdriver in his hand was pointed straight at the creature. Its 'eyes' glowed an angry red as the sonic vibrations reached it, it reversed with bewildering speed and shot off down the corridor, disappearing into an open grating like a mouse into its hole.

Harry blinked. 'What was it, Doctor? A metal rat?'

The Doctor shook his head. 'Not a rat—a cybermat,' he said, unconsciously dropping into rhyme. Refusing to say another word, he went on with his work.

Communications Technician Warner's head was nodding over his instrument console. He was nearing the end of his tour of duty, and could think only of the few hours of sleep he would be allowed before the remorseless schedule of Nerva Beacon summoned him back to duty. At least this last hour should be a quiet one. Unless there was an emergency, no more spaceships were due to approach the Beacon during this watch. But the silence made it all the harder to keep awake. Suppose there *was* an emergency, and it found him sleeping? Slipping imperceptibly into sleep, Warner began to dream that he'd slept through an emergency call and was being court-martialled. In the confused jumble of his dream he heard a voice, and realised with a shock that the voice was real.

'I am calling Nerva Beacon. Can anyone hear me? I am calling Nerva Beacon ...' The voice was thick, throaty, somehow alien, even beneath the distorting crackle of the static.

Warner jerked awake, shook his head to clear it and reached for his console. 'Hullo, this is Nerva Beacon. Do you read me?'

The harsh alien voice came through again. 'I hear you. Is that Nerva Beacon?' The voice was faint and crackling, almost inaudible.

Warner adjusted his controls to try and improve reception. 'I read you, but very faintly. Please return to one-two-seven decimal three-five and repeat your message.' He made further adjustments, listened, but heard only the crackle of static. A shadow fell across the console and Warner looked up. Kellman was standing behind him, his face curiously set and intent. Warner fiddled with his controls, got nothing but more static, and gave up. He glanced at Kellman. 'This new asteroid of yours, Professor, are you sure there's no life on it?'

'On Voga? Of course not. How can there be?'

Warner punched up a picture of the asteroid on his vision scanner. The asteroid hung in space, its scarred and pitted surface dark and mysterious. 'I just picked up a call—and *that's* the only place it could have come from.'

Kellman sneered. 'Hallucinations, Warner. You've been sitting here too long.'

Warner yawned and rubbed his eyes. He nodded towards the scanner screen. 'Where did that thing come from?'

'Nobody knows. It drifted into our system years ago. They detected it when it was captured by Jupiter.'

'So there *could* be life on it?' persisted Warner.

Kellman gave a snort of irritation. 'Impossible,' he said loftily. 'An asteroid that size, drifting in the vacuum between star systems ... nothing could have lived under those conditions.'

Warner was unshaken. 'Well, something did, because that's where that transmission came from.'

Kellman gave an impatient sigh. 'Warner, I'm the exologist, remember? I've been down on Voga. I've set up a transmat station. I've spent six months studying rock samples from Voga ... What are you doing?'

Warner's hands were flickering over a small keyboard. Lettering appeared on a mini-screen in front of him 'Unidentified call from Voga. 18.57 hours. Day 3. Week 47.' Warner replied, 'I'm putting the transmission in my log. Standard procedure.'

'You're mad,' snarled Kellman. 'I've said all along it was a mistake to keep this control-room operative.'

Warner looked at him in astonishment, puzzled by the violence of Kellman's reaction. 'That's the Commander's decision. Nothing to do with you, is it?'

Kellman seemed to calm down a little. 'This place is away from the safe area. Every time you go down that perimeter corridor you risk spreading the plague. We should shut down completely.'

Warner looked hard at him. 'Then why are you here

so often? Anyway, if the Commander says we stay operational, we stay operational.'

Kellman seemed about to speak, changed his mind, turned and stalked from the room. Warner shrugged and returned to his watch, checking the space-radar screen for activity. There was nothing. He yawned again. Not long to go now, and Lester would relieve him. Vaguely he wondered why Kellman had found the idea of transmissions from Voga so upsetting.

Back in the perimeter corridor, the Doctor had at last managed to remove a panel in the door that barred their way. He reached through and groped for the controls on the other side. 'If one of you would hold the door so it doesn't open too suddenly ...' Obligingly Harry Sullivan leaned his weight against the door. The Doctor touched the unseen control-panel. 'That's the idea, Harry. I'm very attached to my humerus, and I'd hate to lose it.' Harry felt the door start to slide back. Hastily the Doctor pulled his arm out of the panel, nodded to Harry who stood back, and the door slid open. Sarah looked down the corridor ahead, vastly relieved that there seemed to be no more corpses. They all stepped past the door and the Doctor operated the controls to close it behind them. Cautiously they moved on their way.

In his control-room, Warner jerked awake once more, as one of the dials in front of him began to flicker. He leaned forward and spoke into the intercom. 'Hullo, Commander? Listen, sir, somebody has just operated the shutter in the aft perimeter corridor. I know it's impossible, but it's happened. The information's right here on the electronic register.'

The Commander's voice came back through the speaker. 'All right, Warner, we'll check it out.'

In the crewroom Lester and Stevenson looked blankly at each other. Lester shook his head in puzzlement. 'Everybody in that aft section had the plague, Commander. There *can't* be anyone still alive.'

Stevenson nodded. 'I sealed the connecting doors myself. Well, we'd better check the corridor.' He went to a wall locker, took out two hand-blasters and gave one to Lester. 'Just in case.' They both went out.

In the control-room, Warner stared at his dials and wondered what was going on. Forgotten on the screen, the asteroid Voga hung mysteriously in space.

Although he didn't know it, Warner had been right about the transmission. It had come from Voga. In a control-room deep inside that planet, the alien operator who had made it was slumped dead over his instruments. Blaster in hand, another alien creature, obviously some kind of security guard, stood watching over the body of the fellow-Vogan he had just killed.

Two more Vogans strode into the room. Like the guard and the dead radio-operator, they were humanoid in form, with high-domed foreheads and dark-furred faces. Their eyes were large and luminous, like those of creatures accustomed to the dark, and the lighting in the room would have been uncomfortably dim for human eyes. Unlike the overalled radio-operator and the grimly-uniformed guard, the two new arrivals wore the clothes of high-ranking officials, with elaborate robes and high-collared ceremonial cloaks. Their boots, their belt-clasps, their chains of office and insignia, all had the dull yellow gleam of solid gold.

Vorus, the bigger and more senior of the two Vogans, prodded the body of the radio-operator with the tip of one golden boot. It slumped to the floor like a rag-filled sack. His bulging, luminous eyes swung round on to the guard, who stood rigidly to attention. 'You did well. You will be suitably rewarded. Now take this thing away and bury it. Bury it deep.'

As the guard dragged the body away, Magrik, Vorus's assistant, came deferentially forward, recoiling from his leader's angry glare. 'Why?' growled Vorus. 'Why did he do it?'

Timidly Magrik said, 'Perhaps your plan frightened him, Vorus. Indeed, it often frightens me.'

'But you would not have warned the humans. You feel no kinship with them?'

Hastily Magrik said, 'Oh no, no indeed. It is just that so many things may go wrong ...'

Vorus mastered his impatience. Magrik was a timid fool, even for a Vogan, but he was also a scientific genius, and Vorus needed him. The big Vogan put a powerful arm round Magrik's thin shoulders.

'Never fear, Magrik. The plan is a great one and it will work. You and I will *make* it work. When the time is right, Nerva Beacon will be shattered into drifting space-dust.'

'But can we trust our agent?'

'We can trust his greed,' growled Vorus contemptuously. He tapped the huge buckle on his cloak. 'Gold *buys* humans, Magrik, and we have more gold here on Voga than in the rest of the galaxy.'

'If our agent is trustworthy, why has he not. communicated?' persisted Magrik timidly.

'It is better that he should not. By now the Cybermen may be monitoring our radio-link.'

Magrik shuddered. 'The very mention of Cybermen fills me with unspeakable dread.'

Vorus's voice was unexpectedly kind. 'You feel fear because you have lived too long in darkness. When I lead our people into the light, all these ancient fears will drop away. We shall destroy the Cybermen.'

Magrik nodded eagerly. 'You are right, Vorus, I know it. If only I did not feel so afraid ...'

Warner's head nodded as he struggled desperately to stay awake. His relief was overdue now. Wryly he told himself that it was his own fault. If he hadn't sent Lester and the Commander off on some wild-goose chase ... He wondered how they were getting on, if they'd found anything.

From a floor-level grating the metallic, rat-like shape of a Cybermat slid silently into the room. It swivelled round as if scanning, and its electronic eyes glowed red as it fixed on Warner. It glided closer, reared up and launched itself like a rocket at Warner's throat. Warner was briefly aware of a silvery flashing through the air, then something cold and metallic struck him in the throat, and he felt agonising twin stabs of pain in his neck. Reeling, he flung the thing away from him. The Cybermat crashed against the wall, slid to the floor, then, apparently unharmed, scurried back into its grating.

Warner felt a burning fever spread through his veins. His blood seemed to be on fire, and there was a roaring in his ears. He lurched towards the alarm switch, but before he could reach it the roaring blackness swallowed him up and he slumped to the floor.

Kellman appeared in the doorway. He looked down at Warner's body, but made no attempt to help him. With a smile of quiet satisfaction, he crossed to the control console, opened a panel, took out the day's log-tape cassette and dropped it into his pocket. Without giving Warner a second glance, he walked quickly from the room.

Lester and Commander Stevenson stood looking in puzzlement at the connecting door that the Doctor had opened some time earlier. Stevenson examined the area around the missing panel. 'The rivets have been taken out from the other side.'

Lester seemed confused. 'But how, sir? They're blind-headed, nothing to give any purchase.'

'Then they must have been loosened with a sonic vibrator!'

'That's pretty sophisticated technology, sir. We've nothing like that on the Beacon.'

'Exactly. So Warner was right. Somebody did come through.' Stevenson hefted his blaster-pistol thoughtfully. 'Come on. We'll just have to check section by section. And move quietly.'

The Doctor, Sarah and Harry stood looking round a deserted control-room. Sarah shook her head. 'We're going round in circles. I'm sure we've been here before.'

The Doctor patted her on the shoulder. 'That was the *aft* control—this is the forward area.'

Harry sounded glum. 'Well, wherever it is, still no TARDIS.'

The Doctor grinned reassuringly. 'Don't worry, it'll turn up soon.'

Harry said sceptically, 'It'll just, what d'you call it —*materialise*, will it?'

'That's right. Only we'll have to be around when it does. It won't wait for us, you see, we've got to catch it when it's in our time co-ordinate, or it'll drift on past.'

Sarah had a picture of a phantom TARDIS, for ever bobbing on ahead of them, always just out of reach. 'Worse than trying to catch a London bus,' she grumbled.

Two men carrying ugly-looking blasters leaped through the doorway, aiming the weapons straight at them. The Doctor ignored the interruption. 'Anyway, when it does arrive ...'

The older of the two men snapped, 'Get your hands up!'

'Certainly,' said the Doctor amiably, raising his hands to shoulder height. 'As I was saying, Harry, when the TARDIS *does* arrive ...'

Obviously taken aback at being totally ignored, the younger man shouted, 'Who are you? How did you get here?'

The Doctor performed introductions, with all the aplomb of a vicar at a garden party. 'This is Miss Sarah Jane Smith, this young man is Harry Sullivan and I'm the Doctor. And you are?'

'My name's Lester. This is Commander Stevenson. I want to know . . .'

A third man appeared in the doorway. Stevenson didn't seem pleased to see him. 'What do you want, Professor Kellman? We're a little busy at the moment.'

Kellman looked curiously at the three new arrivals and said, You'd better come to the sub-control-room, Commander. There's an emergency.'

Stevenson hesitated, then waved his blaster at the captives. 'All right, you three, move. You're coming with us.'

A few minutes later they were all standing in a smaller control-room, where the body of a man lay slumped on the floor. Stevenson gasped, 'Warner!' Gently he turned the body over. A network of spidery black lines ran up from the man's throat, covering one side of his face almost to the temple.

The Commander stood up, his face grim and set. He gave Lester an agonised look. Lester said, 'You want me to do it, sir?'

Stevenson shook his head. 'No. It's my job.' He slid back the bolt of his blaster and took careful aim at Warner's head.

Sarah rushed forward. 'What are you doing? You mustn't!'

'This man has contracted space plague. There's only one way to deal with it.'

'But he's ill—he needs treatment.'

'There is no treatment. All we can do is stop the plague spreading further. I *must* shoot him.'

# 3

# A Hot Spot for the Doctor

Calmly the Doctor stepped forward, placing himself between Stevenson's blaster and the body on the floor. 'I'm sorry,' he said gently, 'I can't possibly allow you to do that.' Such was the authority in the Doctor's voice, that Stevenson found himself lowering his blaster, without quite realising why.

'*You* can't allow it,' he said slowly. 'And just who might you be?'

'I happen to be a doctor. So is my colleague here. Miss Smith is our assistant.'

Suddenly Kellman broke in, 'You'd better kill all three of them, Commander. They've carried the plague into this section.'

The Doctor gave him a look of some distaste, then turned back to Stevenson. 'Commander, who *is* this homicidal maniac?'

Stevenson ignored the question, staring at the Doctor with sudden hope. 'You say you're doctors? Did Earth Centre send you?'

'We're from Earth, yes,' said the Doctor, feeling he could be excused a little evasiveness in the circumstances. 'The important thing is that we've come to help you.' He knelt by Warner's body.

Again Kellman interrupted. 'Help us? Do you realise you've carried the infection from the aft section into *here*?'

Sarah was no scientist, but even she could see the

fallacy in this. 'Use your common sense. If we carried the infection, how come this poor man's ill—and we aren't? He was here before us.'

Harry added his support. 'Maybe the virus hopped off us and dashed in here ahead, eh?'

The Doctor got slowly to his feet. 'Whatever's attacking this man, and all the others—it isn't plague, Commander.'

Stevenson rubbed a hand over his forehead, fighting off a sudden wave of fatigue. 'Well, according to our medical team it is.'

'Did they manage to identify the virus?' asked the Doctor.

Lester shook his head. 'They didn't get much chance. All the medical people went down with plague first.'

'Did they now? Don't you find that rather significant?'

'We reckoned maybe it started in their labs. Some virus mutating in a test-tube.'

'I very much doubt it,' said the Doctor briskly. 'Well, now you've got a new medical team. Dr Sullivan, will you see to the patient? I wish to continue my investigations.'

Commander Stevenson felt that everything was being taken out of his hands. Whoever this odd-looking stranger was, he didn't lack assurance. Half-resentful, half-relieved he said, 'All right, I'll allow you to examine him. It'll have to be in the crewroom though. This control-room *must* be kept operational.'

This produced another outburst from Kellman. 'Oh yes—we must keep operational at *all* costs!' Aware that everyone was staring at him, he turned and strode from the room.

28

Stevenson slid into Warner's seat behind the console. 'Lester, you look after the doctors. I'll take over the console, you relieve me when you can.'

Lester, Harry and Sarah carried the unconscious Warner out of the room. Mechanically, Stevenson started checking over his instrument panel. The Doctor wandered round the room, as if he didn't quite know what he was looking for, stooping to examine some tiny scratches on wall and floor.

(In his tiny metal walled room, Kellman sat hunched over a listening device. It had been a simple matter to 'bug' the control-room, and now he wanted to know what this too-knowing stranger was up to. The voices of the Doctor and Stevenson came through quite clearly.)

The Doctor found yet another tiny scratch on the edge of the instrument console. 'Have you noticed these rather strange scratches, Commander? They seem to crop up all over your base.'

'I can't say I have. Is it important?'

The Doctor smiled. 'Everything's important, Commander, in its own way.' Leaning over Stevenson's shoulder he flicked open the access panel to the log-recording section. He looked at the row of cassettes— with their obvious gaps. 'Well, well, well ... Do you know, Commander, I've already made three interesting discoveries about this plague virus of yours?'

Stevenson looked up. 'Three discoveries?'

The Doctor nodded solemnly. 'One, it can scratch metal. Two, it attacks so suddenly that the victims can't reach an alarm just a few feet away. Three, it steals tape cassettes from log-books. An acquisitive and literate little virus, wouldn't you say?'

Wearily Stevenson shook his head, trying to take it all in. 'Just what are you telling me, Doctor?'

'As I said before—some hostile force is attacking your crew members. But it certainly isn't any kind of plague.'

'Then what is it?'

The Doctor wasn't quite ready to answer that question. He took refuge in a sudden change of subject. 'Who's that singularly unpleasant civilian of yours?'

Stevenson explained about Kellman, and his role in studying the new asteroid, Voga. He was quite unprepared for the violence of the Doctor's reaction.

'That's it—Voga!' shouted the Doctor, smacking himself on the forehead with a blow like a pistol-shot. 'Of course!'

'Of course, *what*?'

'This chap Kellman—has he actually been down there?'

'Yes, of course. He spent some time studying the thing. He even set up a transmat station to link the Beacon and Voga.'

'Voga,' said the Doctor slowly. 'The legendary Voga, the planet made of gold. This makes it certain—they must be involved.'

'Who must?'

The Doctor looked at him, his face suddenly grave. 'I'm sorry to have to tell you, Commander, that we're up against the Cybermen.'

The name rang only the faintest of bells in Stevenson's mind. Some legendary war, long centuries ago ... There had been so many enemies when Man first ventured out among the stars. 'We defeated them, didn't we, hundreds of years ago? I thought they'd died out.'

The Doctor shook his head. 'Disappeared, certainly. Most of their ships vanished after the attack on Voga, after the end of the Cyberwar. Not the same as dying out, Commander. They're totally ruthless, with a great determination to survive, and to conquer. They won't have forgiven Mankind . . .'

In his office, Kellman switched off his listening device, and sat brooding for a moment. There was no doubt in his mind that the Doctor knew too much. Two things were clear. The Doctor must be dealt with. And the Master Plan must be brought forward. Kellman went to a hidden locker and produced a communications device of a strange and alien design. He connected it to the Beacon's power line and began tapping out an urgent message.

On one of the moons of Jupiter an alien space-ship lay hidden. Its lines were harsh and ugly, vicious and functional, like everything made by Cybermen. Inside that ship, giant silver figures sat listening to Kellman's message, considering its many implications. No one spoke. All turned and looked at the central figure, the Cyberleader. He would decide. The others would obey without question. The Cyberleader raised his hand in an abrupt gesture of decision. One of the crew stretched out a giant hand towards the firing levers, and the countdown began. Minutes later the Cybership, scarred and battered, but still efficient and deadly, took off from its hiding place and set a course for Nerva Beacon. The Cybermen were on their way.

In the crewroom, Harry Sullivan looked up from the unconscious figure of Warner and shook his head, 'It beats me. He's in a deep coma, but his temperature is shooting up and up.'

Sarah was holding Warner's wrist. 'Harry, I make his pulse a hundred and twenty!'

Lester wasn't surprised. 'It's always the same, Doc. They just seem to burn up. He's lasted longer than most.'

Sarah let go of Warner's wrist. 'How long ago did all this start?'

Lester thought for a moment. 'This must be ... yeah, the seventy-ninth day, I reckon.'

'Didn't they send you any help?'

'Earth Centre decided to isolate us. Better to lose one beacon crew than spread some unknown plague through the galaxy.'

Suddenly Warner choked and twisted. Lester sighed. 'That's about it. That's how all the others went.'

The Doctor and Commander Stevenson hurried into the crewroom. Harry looked up. 'I'm afraid he's beyond help, Doctor.'

The Doctor leaned over Warner, who was moaning and twisting as the fires of his fever consumed him. Gently steadying the man's head, the Doctor produced a magnifying glass and examined Warner's neck. 'You see, Harry—here? Two tiny punctures ...'

Harry peered through the magnifying glass. 'Like the bite of a serpent.'

'Exactly like, Harry. This man's been injected with some kind of venom.'

Warner convulsed in a final paroxysm, went rigid, then lay quite still. The Doctor sighed, and pulled a sheet over his face. As if lost in thought, the Doctor began walking slowly from the room. Harry called after him, 'Doctor, where are you going?'

'Hunting, Harry. I smell a rat.' And with that the Doctor was gone.

Stevenson gave a baffled frown. 'This is all beyond me. But I can tell you one thing. There are no rats on this beacon. Or snakes either, come to that.'

'Don't worry, Commander,' said Sarah solemnly. 'If the Doctor's scented a rat, he'll find one.'

Unsure exactly where to start his rat-hunt, the Doctor walked slowly along the perimeter corridor. He heard a metallic rattle and instinctively flattened himself against the wall. Further down the corridor a door opened, and Kellman emerged, locking the door behind him. He moved off down the corridor, luckily in the direction that took him away from the Doctor.

Never one to ignore a nudge from fate, the Doctor waited till Kellman was out of sight, then slipped cautiously up to his door. A few minutes work with his sonic-screwdriver dealt with the lock, and the Doctor was soon inside Kellman's tiny office.

There wasn't much to look at. A day-bed, a locker, a desk-table, a filing cabinet and a chair. That was it. The Doctor leafed aimlessly through a selection of files, abandoned them, and started tapping the walls. A quick search revealed Kellman's hidden locker. The Doctor examined the communication-device, shivered at its alien design and put it back, closing the locker.

He turned his attention to the big clothes-locker. There was little to see, just the bare minimum of serviceable clothing. An old pair of shoes was stuffed away in one corner. The Doctor lifted them out, one in each hand and hefted them, weighing and comparing. He tipped up the left shoe and a small string-necked bag fell on to the floor. The Doctor picked it up, carried it over to the table and tipped a little of the bag's contents into his palm. The bag held dust, heavy, yellow, metallic dust. The Doctor took a pinch between finger and thumb, rubbing them together. Only one metal in the cosmos had that slippery, almost oily feel.

'Gold,' he said softly. 'Solid gold . . .'

There was a sudden rattle at the door and the handle started moving. Stuffing the bag in his pocket, the Doctor moved too . . .

Outside in the corridor, Kellman wondered why the lock on his door felt suddenly strange and stiff. He forced it open, and entered the room. It was as quiet and empty as when he had left it. He went to the desk and took a small metal box from a drawer. He put the box on to the metal desk-top and then paused. Something seemed slippery between the two metal surfaces. He lifted the box, wetted a finger, ran it along the desk-top. The finger was thinly coated with gold.

Kellman glanced carefully round the room, keeping quite still. There was only one possible hiding-place—under the day-bed. Kellman considered for a moment, then suddenly smiled. He had thought of a way to make things hot for his unseen visitor. He crossed to a wall panel, and lifted it off to expose the controls for the underfloor heating system. He removed some fuses, wrenched out and cross-connected some wires, then left the room, locking the door behind him.

Stretched flat on his face under the day-bed, the

Doctor had had little better than a worm's-eye-view of Kellman, seeing no more than his boots as he'd moved about the room. Conscious that his own position was rather lacking in dignity, he was very relieved when Kellman went out. The Doctor waited a moment longer, just in case of a sudden return, gazing abstractedly at the plastic-composition floor a few inches beneath his nose. He noticed something very odd about that floor. It was smoking. Indeed, it was starting to bubble and crack. The Doctor shot out from under the bed like a scalded cat and jumped on top of it. The floor of the room was hissing and bubbling like molten larva. Blasts of heat and choking smoke were wafting up from it. The Doctor wound his scarf over his mouth and leaned awkwardly over to try to reach the lock of the door. Little spurts of flickering flame began blossoming in the molten plastic, like yellow flowers.

Sarah Jane Smith sat on her own in the crewroom. Harry and Lester were carrying Warner's body off to the mortuary section. She'd accepted eagerly when Lester had offered her a meal before leaving, but now she was picking unenthusiastically through a plastic box of food concentrates, most of which looked like pink Oxo cubes, and tasted unimaginable. She realised that the crew had been living on pills and concentrates so long they took it for granted, and she thought longingly of steak and chips.

She didn't notice when the triangular silvery form of the Cybermat slipped out of its grating, red eyes glowing as it sought its prey. This time it managed to glide so close that by the time she saw it there was no chance of escape, no time even to scream as the Cyber-mat reared up and launched itself at her throat . . .

In Kellman's office, the automatic sprinkler system was struggling to put out the fire. The Doctor heaved the metal desk across the bubbling, burning floor to the door, falling forward like a bridge, feet on the bed, one hand supporting him on the desk. In this position, he could—just—reach the lock with the sonic-screwdriver in his other hand. Working one-handed, his weight bearing agonisingly on his sup-porting wrist, waves of stifling heat and choking black smoke coming up at him from the blazing floor, the Doctor felt like a chop on a barbecue griddle. Under these conditions it was a much tougher job to pick the lock, and the Doctor felt consciousness slipping away as he inhaled the fumes of burning plastic. The door sprang open at last, and the Doctor vaulted over the desk to land in a heap in the metal-floored corridor outside. As he picked himself up, he heard the sound of Sarah's screams. Gasping for breath, the Doctor stag-gered along the corridor towards the sound.

After the shock of seeing the Cybermat jump at her, Sarah had got her breath back and was screaming at the top of her voice. The Cybermat seemed clamped to her throat, and she felt twin stabs of agonising pain in her neck. With a final desperate effort, she wrenched it away, hurling it across the room—to land at the feet of the Doctor as he appeared in the doorway. The Cybermat spun round, orientating itself. Its eyes glowed red as they fixed upon this new victim. Rear-ing up, it prepared to launch itself at the Doctor . . .

# 4

## A Visit to Voga

The Doctor sidestepped nimbly as the Cybermat jumped. It crashed into the wall beside his head, dropped to the floor, spun round to get its bearings and reared to attack again.

Groping in his pockets, the Doctor backed away. Just as the creature was about to spring, the Doctor fished out the bag of gold-dust from Kellman's room, and tipped the lot over the Cybermat. The result was extraordinary. The creature spun round and round in a kind of frenzy, sending off a whirling spray of gold-dust. At last it juddered to a halt. The red eyes glowed even more fiercely, then went dark. The Cybermat was still.

With the immediate danger past, the Doctor became aware that Sarah was staggering towards him. Appalled, he saw the lines of spidery black markings that were already running from her neck up to her temple. She reeled and fell, clutching her throat and making guttural, choking sounds. The Doctor caught her just before she hit the floor. He was lifting her on to a bunk as Harry, Lester and the Commander raced into the room.

Harry hurried over to Sarah. 'What happened? We heard the screams.'

Lester took one look at Sarah and said grimly, 'We're too late. She's got the plague.'

'There *is* no plague,' said the Doctor. 'Only this.'

He kicked the immobilised Cybermat. It was distorted, almost melted by the effect of the gold-dust, and looked like a lump of shapeless metal scrap. 'It's programmed to inject some alien poison into the bloodstream of its victims.'

Stevenson examined it with revulsion. 'Is it still dangerous, Doctor?'

'Not any more. But there are bound to be others around.' The Doctor crossed over to Harry, who was trying to soothe the writhing, gasping Sarah. Harry was very much aware that on this self-same bunk, just a short time ago, he had watched Warner die, powerless to help him. He turned his agonised face to the Doctor.

'There must be something we can do for her.'

The Doctor stood looking down at Sarah. He seemed lost in contemplation. You could almost hear the whirring as his brain raced through a variety of possible solutions. Suddenly he snapped his fingers. 'There is, Harry. The transmat beam in the control-room!'

Harry gaped at him. His travels with the Doctor had familiarised him with this latest triumph of man's technology, an apparatus that could break down a living human body into a stream of molecules, send it to a predetermined destination by a locked transmitter beam, and reassemble it unharmed at the other end. With transmat you could send a person as easily as a telephone message. But how could that help Sarah?

'Don't you see,' said the Doctor urgently. 'The transmat disperses human molecules. The alien poison will be separated and rejected, and when Sarah arrives she'll be cured. Come on, Harry!' Ignoring the others, they started to carry Sarah from the room. Automatically, Lester and the Commander followed after them.

A few minutes later, Harry was supporting Sarah as they both stood inside the small plain cubicle which was the Beacon terminal for the transmat beam. The Doctor was at the nearby control console.

'Now you know what to do, Harry? The minute you arrive, use the reciprocator switch, and you'll be beamed straight back again. We don't know what's on Voga, and it could be dangerous to spend much time there.'

Harry nodded. 'Don't worry. We'll be there and back as soon as this thing can take us.' He tightened his grip on Sarah protectively. The Doctor's hands flickered over the controls. Nothing happened. He tried again. Still nothing. The Doctor ripped the back-panel from the transmat control console and stared into the intricate tangle of electronic equipment. Lester peered over his shoulder.

'Has it broken down, Doctor?'

'No. This isn't a breakdown. It's sabotage. Somebody's removed the main power-source, the pentalion drive.'

Commander Stevenson was incredulous. 'Sabotage? Who'd do a thing like that?'

'Who tore the tape from your radio-log?' asked the Doctor savagely. 'Who used Cybermats to murder your crew? Who's desperate to cut all connection between this Beacon and Voga?'

Commander Stevenson knew exactly who the Doctor meant. 'Kellman?'

'Kellman!' confirmed the Doctor. 'Your friendly exographer is working with the Cybermen.'

That was enough for Lester. He rubbed his big hands together. 'Come on, Commander, let's get after him.'

Lester and Stevenson hurried out of the room, reaching for the blasters in their belts.

(In his fire-ruined office, Kellman took his ear from his listening device and hurriedly started to leave. He took the small metal box from his drawer, and opened it. Inside was a compact, complicated piece of electronic equipment—the missing pentalion drive. Kellman tucked it into a concealed pocket inside his tunic, took a mini-blaster from the drawer and put it in another pocket, then quickly left the room.)

The Doctor made no attempt to join Stevenson and Lester in their hunt for Kellman. He was still peering into the recesses of the transmat controls, talking almost to himself, as he carefully detached a small wire-trailing cylinder from one of the subsidiary circuits. 'This might work at a pinch,' he muttered. 'If I can adapt the monophode to a three-phase output . . .'

From the transmat booth Harry Sullivan called, 'Hurry, Doctor, she's dying, just like Warner. It's happening all over again.' The Doctor looked up. Sarah had stopped struggling now, and lay limply against Harry. The spider web network of black lines covered nearly all her face, and her body felt hot to the touch.

'Just hold on, old chap,' said the Doctor gently. 'I'll be as quick as I can.' He fished a watchmaker's eyeglass from his pocket, and screwed it in his eye. Then he took a jeweller's screwdriver from another pocket. Slowly, and with infinite patience, he began undoing the tiny screws that held the cylinder together.

By the time the Commander and Lester had blasted the lock from Kellman's door and rushed inside, there was no sign of the missing exographer. 'Skipped,' said Lester angrily.

The Commander glanced round the still smoke-filled room. 'And in a hurry, by the look of things. All right, let's get after him.' In the corridor outside, Stevenson paused. 'You take that section down there, Lester. I'll check the perimeter corridor.' The two men split up. Blasters at the ready, they moved cautiously on their way.

The Doctor meanwhile had finished his improvised drive mechanism, and was hoping desperately that it would be strong enough to provide the power-surge. He called across to Harry. 'There isn't time to wire this in properly, I'll have to hold it in. Stand by.' One hand holding the cylinder in place, the Doctor used the other to manipulate the controls. There was a hum of power, the transmat booth lit up, and Harry and Sarah dematerialised. The Doctor grinned triumphantly. Almost immediately there was a bang and a flash from the transmat control console, and the Doctor snatched out his hand. He jumped up and down sucking his fingers. His improvised circuit had got Sarah and Harry to the meteorite Voga. But how was he going to get them back again?

As Commander Stevenson crept carefully along the perimeter corridor, he heard stealthy movement ahead. The sound seemed to be coming towards him. Stevenson flattened himself against the corridor wall and waited. When the footsteps had almost reached him, he stepped out into the corridor, blaster raised. He found himself facing Kellman. But Kellman was holding a blaster too, and it was aimed straight at *him*.

Kellman gave his familiar sneer. 'Go ahead and fire, Commander. At this range, neither of us will miss.'

Feeling rather foolish, Stevenson snapped, 'Drop that blaster, Kellman, you won't get away.'

Blaster aimed steadily at Stevenson's midriff, Kellman groped along the corridor wall behind him with his other hand, until he found the handle of a door. 'I'm going into this cabin, Commander. Lock me in if you like, or put a guard on the door. Just don't try to come in. You'll soon have a lot more than me to worry about.'

Kellman opened the door, and was about to slip inside when Lester came running down the corridor. The momentary distraction was enough. Instinctively Kellman swung his blaster towards the new arrival, and Stevenson promptly jumped him, grabbing his wrist and wrenching the blaster downwards. Lester joined in the struggle, and within minutes Kellman was disarmed and overpowered. None too gently, Stevenson and Lester dragged him off down the corridor.


In the transmat cubicle in a tunnel deep inside Voga, Harry flicked frantically at the reciprocator switch that was supposed to return them to Nerva Beacon. Sarah, cured but confused, stood beside him watching his efforts. Since she had no memory of what had happened between her being 'bitten' by the Cybermat and recovering consciousness on Voga, she had been understandably taken aback to find herself in a transmat cubicle in a dimly-lit mining gallery. The Doctor's unorthodox cure had certainly worked. The spider web lines had disappeared from her face, her temperature was back to normal and she was completely her old self again. She was well enough to get very impatient with standing in a cubicle watching Harry Sullivan struggle with a useless switch. 'For goodness' sake, Harry, how long are we going to stand here?'

'Until this thing starts working again. Strict instructions from the Doctor. We're staying here.'

'I wouldn't be too sure of that, Harry.' There was something different in the tone of Sarah's voice, and Harry looked up. Two bulging-eyed, dome-headed humanoid creatures in military uniforms were standing over them, blasters aimed. Harry sighed, and slowly raised his hands.

Meanwhile, in the control-room back on Nerva Beacon, Kellman, battered but still defiant, was glaring at his three captors in obstinate silence. The Doctor waved towards the picture of Voga, still punched up on the vision screen. 'There's Voga, you see, Commander, what remains of it, and not far away, I fancy, are what remain of the Cybermen.'

Lester scratched his head. 'You mean the Cybermen followed that rock into our star system—why?'

'To destroy it. That meteorite is all that's left of Voga, once known as the Planet of Gold. The planet was broken up by the Cybermen, just before their defeat in the Cyberwar. They can't rest till this last fragment is shattered too.'

'Why is it so important to them?' asked Stevenson.

The Doctor's voice was solemn. 'Because the Cybermen hate gold. It's lethal to them. It's the perfect non-corrodable metal. It plates their breathing apparatus, and, in effect, suffocates them. Doesn't it, Professor?'

Kellman made no reply. He gazed straight ahead, a faint sneer on his face. The Doctor's tall figure loomed over him menacingly. 'My two friends, Harry and Sarah, are stranded on Voga, thanks to you. I can't bring them back without the pentalion drive. Where is it?'

Kellman still didn't speak. The Doctor turned to Lester. 'You said you searched his cabin after you caught him?'

Lester nodded. He pointed to a jumble of equipment on top of one of the control panels. 'That's all we found.'

The Doctor looked at the pile. 'Yes, I saw that earlier. Equipment to contact his masters, more equipment to spy on his colleagues. But what have you done with the pentalion drive, Kellman?'

For the first time, Kellman deigned to reply. 'I'm sorry, I've no idea what you're talking about.'

The Doctor looked at him thoughtfully. 'You're lying, Professor, I'm sure of that. But why?' He wandered to the pile of Kellman's equipment, and began idly sorting through it. He fished a little box from beneath the pile and turned it over in his hands. Complex controls were set into one side.

Irritably Kellman snapped, 'What are you doing? That's part of my surveying equipment. Leave it alone.'

The Doctor ignored him, and went on idly fiddling with the little box. He glanced at Lester and Stevenson. 'I think our mercenary friend here is lying to gain

44

time. But time for what, I wonder?'

Kellman shot him a look of pure hatred, but made no reply. He seemed unable to take his eyes from the box in the Doctor's hands.

On the control-deck of the Cybermen's space-ship, the leader was listening to a report from his engineer. In his sibilant, whispering voice the engineer said, 'Computer reports energy-discharge between Nerva Beacon and Voga.' There was no emotion in the mechanical voice. Cybermen do not have feelings.

The Cyberleader's reply was equally toneless. 'Then the humans have used their transmat beam?'

'The inference is logical, leader.'

'That was not in the plan. Time to docking?'

'Sixteen minutes, leader.'

The silver giant rose to his feet, towering in the space-ship cabin. 'Order the boarding party to the forward hatch. I shall lead the attack myself.'

In the ornately decorated Guild Room on Voga, Vorus sat brooding behind his massive desk. After a moment, the big golden doors swung open and Magrik scurried in. He stood nervously before the desk, and bowed his head. 'You sent for me?'

Vorus said flatly, 'The Cybermen are on the move.'

Immediately Magrik panicked. 'But it is too soon. We are not ready . . .'

'Our agent reported some time ago. Since then, he has been silent. We can wait for news no longer. You have, perhaps, four hours to complete the Skystriker.'

'That is impossible, Vorus!'

'Four hours, no more, Magrik, else all our dreams are ended.'

Desperately Magrik tried to explain. 'The Sky-striker is almost ready, but the bomb has yet to be tested. It will take four hours or more to fit, and with the time for the tests as well . . .'

Vorus rose behind his desk, towering over the little engineer. 'Fit the bomb immediately. It will be tested when it strikes the Beacon. Do you understand?'

Magrik gave a sigh of assent. 'It shall be as you say, Vorus. I will call every available engineer to the bunkers. We shall begin at once.'

As Magrik left, Vorus called after him, 'Tell the guards to bring in the humans who were captured in the tunnels.'

When Harry and Sarah were brought in through the golden doors, Vorus ignored them for a moment or two, carrying on with his work. Flanked by two huge armed security guards, the human captives looked curiously round the richly decorated Guild Room. There were hangings, drapes, shields and ornaments everywhere. Most of them, like the big doors they had just come through, appeared to be made from solid gold. They looked at the humanoid creature behind the desk. It had the same high, dome-shaped forehead and bulging luminous eyes as the guards who had captured them. But the rich robes and the multiplicity of gold ornaments indicated that he was a high-ranking member of this strange underground race.

The waiting began to get on Sarah's nerves. She leaned closer to Harry and whispered, 'Wish he'd get on with it. The Doctor will be worried about us.'

'*I'm* worried about us,' whispered Harry. 'What is this place anyway?'

Sarah looked over her shoulder, and then glanced again at the alien behind the desk. 'I can tell you what it *isn't*—it isn't uninhabited.'

Their whispering irritated Vorus, and he looked up angrily. 'Bring the prisoners to me.' The guards shoved Harry and Sarah forward until they were standing just in front of him. Vorus looked at them coldly. 'So—you are from the Beacon.' It was a statement, not a question. 'Why have you come to Voga? Was it to escape the plague?'

Hesitantly Sarah said, 'Well, yes, it was because of the plague . . .'

Vorus leaped to his feet. 'You lie. The truth is that you came to steal our gold.'

'I'm not lying,' said Sarah spiritedly. 'You see I got the plague and . . .'

'You lie!' shouted Vorus again. 'If you had caught the plague you would be dead by now. That was the plan.'

Vorus was almost incoherent with rage, and they could make little sense of his outburst. Harry seized on the last word of Vorus's speech. 'Plan? You *planned* these deaths?' He sounded almost as angry as the alien.

Sarah tried to calm things down. 'We arrived on the Beacon *after* the plague had started. Then I was bitten, and the Doctor put me in the transmat beam to cure me, didn't he, Harry?'

'That's right. I only came along to help. If the transmat had worked we'd have gone straight back. We've no intention of stealing your ruddy gold.'

Vorus came round his desk and stalked menacingly

47

up to them—like some great cat bearing down on two mice, thought Sarah. His voice was harsh and threatening. 'Why did you come here? How many humans are on the Beacon now? What is their plan? What do they know of us here on Voga?'

Harry and Sarah exchanged glances. Neither of them spoke. Neither had any intention of giving information about Nerva Beacon to these alien creatures, particularly as they seemed to be somehow implicated in the spreading of the faked plague.

Their silence drove Vorus into a frenzy. His eyes seemed to blaze with rage. 'When Vorus, Leader of the Guardians, asks questions, it is not wise to refuse to answer.' Still Harry and Sarah said nothing. Vorus made a sign to the guards who grabbed their arms and twisted them cruelly. 'If you do not answer my questions you will *suffer*,' he hissed. 'When the guards have done with you I shall ask again, and you will be eager to answer me.' At a nod from Vorus the guards twisted harder, and Sarah and Harry both gasped in pain. Vorus smiled cruelly. 'Well, *humans*—are you ready to speak?'

# 5

# Rebellion!

Sarah felt as if her arm was being torn from its socket. She clenched her teeth in an effort not to scream. Dimly, she was aware of Harry, struggling to break free from his guard. Suddenly a melodious chime rang through the council chamber. Immediately the scene froze. Everyone stopped moving. It was obvious that the chime had great importance for the Vogans. It rang out again, louder and more imperious. Vorus waved angrily at the guards. 'Remove them. Take them to the place of confinement. I will question them later.' Sarah and Harry were dragged out.

Vorus waited until the golden doors had closed behind them, then touched a control-button on his desk. One wall slid completely away to reveal a giant screen. The picture on the wall showed a room, smaller and far simpler than the one in which Vorus stood. It was bare and functional, completely without ostentation. In it another Vogan sat working at a simple table. He was small and slender, dressed in plain dark robes. He looked out of the screen at Vorus and said mildly, 'Ah, there you are, Vorus. There are matters of importance I must discuss with you.'

Vorus frowned. 'Indeed, Councillor Tyrum?' He waited expectantly.

'Not over the vision-projector,' said Tyrum. 'You must come to me here, in the city.'

'I am not aware of any matters of such urgency . . .'

'But I am,' interrupted Tyrum calmly. 'As always, Vorus, I look forward to our meeting with the keenest pleasure. I am sending our fastest skimmer to collect you.' He touched a control and the screen went dark, leaving Vorus glaring angrily at its blankness. For the hundredth time, Vorus wondered how Tyrum always made him feel so ineffectual. The summons was worrying, coming at such a crucial time. Nevertheless, Vorus dared not disobey. One of Tyrum's gentle requests had the force of a royal command. For all his mildness, Tyrum was someone to be reckoned with. As President of the High Council, he was the most powerful being on all Voga. Resentfully, Vorus began making preparations for his journey. The interrogation of the two captive humans would have to wait.

Harry and Sarah were taken to a cave just off one of the main tunnels. It was damp and dark, the walls and roof festooned with long, spear-like stalactites. Roughly the guards fastened them to chains set into the rock walls, then left without a word. Sarah slumped despondently against the wall, struggling in vain to find a comfortable position. Harry looked around him with keen interest. 'I say, old girl, look at those glittering bits in these rocks. All top-grade ore, that. We're prisoners in a gold mine.'

Sarah wriggled into a new position, and found it even less comfortable. 'That's great. If they leave us here, we'll die rich.'

Harry clanked his chains experimentally. 'These chains are gold too—seems to be the only metal they use.'

'Harry, will you shut up about the rotten gold?' muttered Sarah crossly.

'Twenty-four carat, I should think,' Harry added.

'Harry, please. It's because of the gold that we're *in* this mess. The stuff's no use to us, is it?'

'It might be,' said Harry mysteriously.

'How?'

'What I mean is, gold's a pretty soft metal, you see. If we can find a decent bit of rock we might be able to break these chains.'

Sarah cheered up at the prospect of action. 'Well, I suppose it's worth a try. Can't just sit here counting our money, can we?'

By slumping into a painful half-sitting position, they found they could just about reach the rock floor beneath them. After some painful contortions, Harry managed to get his hands on a piece of rock about the size of a grapefruit. Using it as a crude hammer, he started bashing away at Sarah's leg-chains with rather more enthusiasm than care.

'Hey, watch it,' yelled Sarah, as a particularly vigorous thump caught her a painful crack on the shin.

'Sorry, old girl,' panted Harry. 'Difficult to get a good aim all twisted round like this.' He peered at the gold loop round Sarah's ankle. 'I think I'm flattening it, though.'

'You're flattening me, more like it. Be a bit more careful.'

'All in a good cause,' said Harry cheerfully. He hammered away determinedly, ignoring Sarah's occasional yells of protest. At last he stopped and took another look. 'You know, I think you could almost get your foot free now. Give it a try.'

He pulled off Sarah's shoe and took a grip on her leg-chain. Sarah tugged her leg back with all the force she could manage. The ankle-loop still felt agonisingly tight.

'Go on, heave,' said Harry encouragingly.

'It hurts!'

'Don't wory about that, just keep on pulling. If you didn't have fetlocks like a horse ...'

'My ankles are *not* thick,' gasped Sarah indignantly. She gave a final angry heave, and her foot came free.

'Well done,' said Harry. 'Now let's have a go at the other one.'

The second loop came free far more easily, the wrist-loops followed, and soon Sarah was out of her chains altogether. She stood and stretched luxuriously, rubbing her wrists and ankles in turn.

'Don't just stand there,' reminded Harry. 'Have a go at getting mine off.'

Sarah looked round. 'Hang on, I've a better idea.' She crossed to a jutting spear of rock, and after a struggle managed to snap it free from its base. 'Now if we use this as a chisel and the rock as a hammer ...'

With the improved tools the work went much more quickly, and soon Harry was standing free beside Sarah, though not without sustaining a few bruises in the process. He hopped about protestingly. 'Oh my goodness. I think I'm maimed for life.'

'I don't know what you're complaining about, the way you whacked at me ... sshh!'

They both heard a low humming noise, coming nearer. Harry grabbed Sarah's hand. 'Come on—we'd better run for it!'

They dashed out of the cave and ran full speed down the mine galleries.

A few minutes later, a hover-car full of security

guards pulled up outside the caves, and an armed guard came in to check on the prisoners. He saw the broken chains and called his squad. They jumped out of the car and began a methodical search for the missing captives.

Commander Stevenson had been hammering away at Kellman for what seemed ages now, but the prisoner showed no signs of breaking down. He sat slumped on a stool, gazing straight ahead, either ignoring the Commander's questions, or at best making some brief, sneering reply. The Doctor was lounging in a corner of the control-room, following the interrogation keenly, but taking no part in it. Lester looked on impatiently. The brawny crewman was wishing that the Commander would turn Kellman over to *him* for a few minutes, let him thump some answers out of the man.

Commander Stevenson, at the end of his patience, decided on tougher measures. He drew his blaster and cocked it, levelling it at Kellman's head. 'Nerva Beacon is on full Red One alert—the equivalent to a time of war. As Station Commander under these conditions, there are certain crimes where I can order immediate execution.'

Kellman gazed ahead, saying nothing.

In a voice shaking with anger Stevenson said, 'You have murdered forty-seven of my men. You have jeopardised the success of this Beacon's mission.'

Kellman glanced up at him. 'You're talking absolute rubbish.'

Stevenson jammed the blaster to Kellman's head.

'What's it going to be, Kellman? Will you tell us where you've hidden the pentalion drive, or do you prefer to die here and now?'

Kellman yawned. 'You're not frightening me, Commander. You won't shoot.'

'I have every right to shoot you here and now——'

'Maybe you have. But you won't do it.' Kellman's voice was quietly complacent. He'd come to know the Commander well during his tour of duty on Nerva Beacon. He knew that Stevenson was simply incapable of shooting him down in cold blood, however great the provocation.

Stevenson knew it too. He sighed and lowered the blaster. With a weary persistence he returned to the attack. He nodded to the little box, still in the Doctor's hands. 'The Doctor says that thing controls the Cybermats.'

For the first time Kellman showed signs of tension. He snapped, 'Well, I say it's an instrument for analysing mineral elements. Every exographer carries one.'

The Doctor spoke for the first time. 'You're still lying, Professor Kellman,' he said mildly.

'Can you prove it?' sneered Kellman.

'Why, yes, I believe I can. I think I've finally got the hang of your little toy.' The Doctor made a few adjustments to the box's controls, and it hummed faintly. Kellman's eyes widened, but he still didn't speak. For a moment nothing happened. Then Lester gave a yell and leaped back as a Cybermat appeared at a duct near his feet, and slid silently into the room. Lester grabbed for the blaster in his belt. But the Cybermat ignored him. It swivelled round on its own axis as if scanning the room, its eyes glowing red. Stevenson aimed his blaster at it, but the Doctor, the box still in his hands, caught his eye and gave an almost imperceptible shake of the head. Stevenson stood quite still. The Cybermat ignored him. It ignored the Doctor too, halting only when it turned to face Kellman, who crouched terrified on his stool in the corner. Remorselessly the Cybermat glided towards him.

Kellman croaked, 'Do something ... for Heaven's sake, one of you stop it!'

Nobody moved. The Doctor, Lester and Stevenson stood silently watching as the Cybermat glided closer and closer to the terrified Kellman. It stopped, just a few inches away from his stool. The Doctor spoke, 'Of course you could still tell me where the pentalion drive is hidden *after* you've been bitten, but you'll be cutting it rather fine. You'll only have a few seconds of consciousness left then, you see, and unless you do manage to tell me, you'll die in agony as the others died.' The Doctor's voice was calm and reasonable, as if explaining an interesting experiment to a class of students.

As the Cybermat reared up for its spring, Kellman's nerve broke. 'All right, all right, I'll tell you,' he screamed. 'It's here round my neck, it was here all the time.' Frantically Kellman's fingers scrabbled at the thin silver chain round his neck, and he tugged a heavy metal locket from inside his shirt. He fumbled with the hidden catch and the locket sprang open to reveal the missing pentalion drive, which he'd hidden in the secret compartment inside.

The Doctor adjusted controls on the little box, and the Cybermat lowered itself to the ground, spun round, whirred and became dormant, the red glow fading slowly from its eyes. Kicking it casually into a corner, the Doctor walked across to Kellman and took the pentalion drive from him. 'Full of little tricks, aren't we?' He looked at the tiny but vital piece of electronic equipment in his palm. 'Still, all's well that ends well. Now we can get Harry and Sarah back!'

The Doctor strode rapidly across to the transmat cubicle, with Lester behind. 'You whistled that thing in, didn't you?' asked Lester admiringly. 'How did you know it would only attack Kellman?'

'Ah, that was the tricky bit. I had to set the controls to home in on his brainwaves.' The Doctor stopped by the transmat control console and peered into its innards thoughtfully. 'Now this is a much more difficult job.' He looked up at Lester solemnly. 'Do you realise, if I put this thing back the wrong way round, the entire Beacon would probably disintegrate?'

Lester gulped and stepped back. 'Ah ... yes. Right then, Doctor, I'll leave you to it.' Lester hurried away. The Doctor grinned and went on with his task.


In the office of Councillor Tyrum, Vorus stood arrogantly before his smaller colleague. He had been kept waiting for some time, and he was in a mood of savage impatience. He spoke with elaborately sarcastic politeness. 'You said a matter of importance, Chief Councillor?'

Tyrum looked infuriatingly blank for a moment, almost as if he'd forgotten why he'd summoned Vorus. 'Ah, yes. I have had a report that two aliens—two humans—have been seen on Voga.'

Vorus thought quickly. Should he confess that the

aliens were his prisoners? No, that was too dangerous. If Tyrum insisted on interrogating the humans, they might tell him of events on the Beacon—and that would mean the end of his great plan. Vorus said nothing.

'By ancient tradition,' continued Tyrum coldly, 'your guards control the upper galleries and the routes to the surface. If humans have set foot on Voga, it must be with your knowledge, even, perhaps, with your connivance.'

Vorus took refuge in bluster. 'You have no proof of these allegations,' he growled.

Placidly Tyrum said, 'Nevertheless, I believe them to be true.' The Councillor moved to a curtained alcove. 'Whatever is happening in the upper galleries, it has not passed unnoticed. Strange stories have reached my ears. Now your guards have resorted to murder— and that I *can* prove!' Tyrum ripped aside the curtain. Behind it, in the alcove, lay the body of the dead radio-operator, killed by Vorus's guard for attempting to send a warning message to Nerva Beacon. 'A squad of your guards was detected attempting to conceal the corpse in the lower galleries.'

Vorus looked at the body, unmoved. 'This does not concern you, Councillor Tyrum. It was a matter of internal discipline.'

For the first time, Tyrum showed signs of anger. 'Does it not? I know your ambitions, Vorus. I know you would have Voga a great power again, trading our gold with the other planets of the galaxy.'

'And why not? Why must we live for ever underground, cowering from the memory of things that happened centuries ago?'

57

'Because this way we *survive*!' Tyrum hammered his fist on the desk. 'In the past our gold brought us greatness, and the greatness in turn brought only sorrow and destruction. We became involved in the Cyberwar, we earned the undying hatred of the Cybermen. Now, while no one suspects that Voga is inhabited, that this is the famous planet of gold—we remain safe.'

Sheer rage overcame Vorus's habitual awe of Tyrum. 'Safe!' he shouted. 'Must we think only of safety? You have the philosophy of a cringing cave-mouse, Tyrum.'

'And you are a gambler with a mad thirst for power. That is why I can no longer trust you and your Guardians. The Council Militia are taking control of the galleries.'

Vorus was outraged. For generations the Guardians, armed troops of the Vogan Guild, had been responsible for the security of the mine galleries that riddled the planet. 'You cannot do this!' he choked.

'It is the lawful decision of the Council. The Militia are moving into the galleries at this very moment. Your men are outnumbered, and the troops will crush any resistance.'

Vorus drew his blaster and strode to the door. 'We shall see,' he growled.

Tyrum leaped to his feet. 'If you resist the lawful decision of the Council, it will be an act of rebellion!'

'Then I rebel!' shouted Vorus. 'And when my rebellion is over, you and your Council will rule Voga no more!'

Angrily he turned and strode from the room.

# 6

# Attack of the Cybermen

The Doctor made a last micro-adjustment to the re-installed pentalion drive, and straightened up, taking the jeweller's eyeglass from his eye and wiping his brow. He replaced the access panel on the console and then operated the controls. There was a satisfactory hum of power, the transmat booth lit up—and nothing happened. The Doctor carried out the transportation procedure again, and yet again. Still no result.

Commander Stevenson came over to him and glanced at the empty cubicle. 'What's the matter, isn't it working?'

'It's working all right. Ticking over on full power. Harry and Sarah must have left the receptor area.' The Doctor noticed Stevenson's worried expression. 'Has something happened?'

'We've picked up a space-ship on our radar-scanners.'

'That's normal enough, surely?' The Doctor went on fiddling with the transmat controls.

'Not this one. There are no more ships due in this section for twelve days And this particular space-ship seems to be heading straight for us.'

'I'll come and take a look.' As the Doctor followed Stevenson he thought to himself that he had a pretty good idea who that space-ship belonged to. Maybe Harry and Sarah were safer where they were.

At that particular moment, Harry and Sarah were running along an endless succession of seemingly identical mine galleries, trying to find their way back to the transmat terminal. Suddenly Harry stopped. 'Listen!'

Sarah listened. A distant rumbling and crackling came from somewhere not far away. 'What is it?'

'Shooting,' said Harry grimly. 'They must be fighting among themselves.'

'That's marvellous. As if we hadn't enough troubles, we have to land up in the middle of a war.'

'Oh no, we don't,' said Harry determinedly. 'We'll stay out of their way and let 'em get on with it.'

They started running away from the direction of the shooting. Unfortunately their chosen route led them straight into a squad of Council Militia, coming up as reinforcements. The Militia instantly covered them with their blasters. Harry sighed and raised his hands. 'Sorry, old girl—but here we go again!'

Outside the Guild Hall, Vorus's Guardians were fighting valiantly, although they were both outnumbered and outweaponed by Tyrum's Militia. The Guardians were driven back and back until they had to make their final stand directly outside the great golden doors.

Sheprah, Captain of the Militia, called, 'Surrender! Further bloodshed is useless.' His only answer was a crackle of blaster fire.

Vorus came out of the Guild Hall and shouted defiantly. 'We shall fight to the last man. No one enters the Guild Hall of the Guardians.'

Sheprah considered. He knew Vorus's Guardians to be fanatically loyal to their chief. Moreover they were well dug in, and he might lose most of his men before he could capture the Guild Hall. He turned to his number two. 'Hold your positions. I shall go and seek orders from Tyrum.'

The Militia settled themselves in for a siege. One or two shots were exchanged, but it was obvious they were making no real attempt to advance further. Vorus went back to the Guild Hall, where he found Magrik waiting in a state of utter panic. Ignoring him, he turned to his military aide. 'We must hold this position at all costs. If Tyrum finds the Skystriker, all our work will have been for nothing.' The Guardian saluted and returned to organise the defence. Vorus turned to Magrik. 'I shall have the two human captives killed at once. If they fall into Tyrum's hands, they might arouse his suspicions of us even further.'

Nervously Magrik stammered, 'That is what I came to tell you. Just before the Militia attacked us, the two humans escaped. By now they may already be in Tyrum's hands.'

Commander Stevenson stood behind Lester as he sat at the control console. On the space-radar screen, a blip of light was moving steadily forward. Stevenson said, 'Have another go at making contact.'

Obediently, Lester flicked his speaker switch. 'This is Nerva Beacon. Nerva Beacon to approaching spacecraft. Do you read me?' There was no reply. The blip of light continued its remorseless progression.

'Try again,' snapped the Commander. 'They're heading straight for us.'

Lester tried again. 'This is Nerva Beacon. You are

approaching Nerva Beacon. We are quarantined with space plague. I repeat, we have plague aboard the Beacon. For your own safety, stand away.'

There was nothing but the crackle of space-static in reply.

'I don't think they'll answer you,' said the Doctor gently. 'Not if they're who I think they are.'

Lester said, 'Look, Commander, they're moving into a docking orbit. I'll see if I can get a visual scanner contact.' Lester manipulated controls, and on a second screen the shape of the space-ship slowly appeared. They all studied it for a moment. It was old and scarred, yet still somehow terrifyingly alien.

Stevenson shook his head. 'Never seen that type before. Have you, Doctor?'

The Doctor nodded. 'I'm afraid I have, a long, long time ago. I hoped never to see one again. Those are Cybermen.'

There was a distant clang, and the Beacon seemed to shudder a little. 'They're docking,' said Lester.

The Doctor was already on his way out of the room. 'Come on, both of you. We've got to stop them getting on board. Where's the airlock?'

The three men ran down the perimeter corridor and into the docking section at the far end. The Doctor opened the massive door to the airlock chamber and looked inside. With a surge of relief he saw that the far door, the one that led to the connection tunnel on to which approaching space-ships must lock, was still closed. The Doctor grabbed Lester by the arm. 'Tools, man. If we can jam the hydraulic control we can still keep them out, at least for a time.'

Lester hauled open a tool locker, while the Doctor

started unclipping an inspection hatch. He lifted it off to reveal a maze of heavy hydraulic piping. Taking a heavy monkey wrench from Lester, the Doctor started to unscrew the main power feed. Or rather he tried to unscrew it. But with the long quarantine period on the Beacon, the docking bay hadn't been used for some time. There had been no proper maintenance since all the engineers were dead. The big locking nut was jammed tight, and nothing the Doctor could do would shift it.

He heaved away desperately, unable to get proper leverage in the confined space. Suddenly Lester tapped his shoulder. 'Doctor, look!'

There was a hiss of pressure and the door of the airlock began to sigh open. 'We're too late,' the Doctor yelled. 'They're coming through!'

He bustled Lester out of the airlock chamber and followed him through the door that led to the corridor, where Commander Stevenson was waiting. Stevenson said urgently, 'What's happening?'

'Cybermen,' said the Doctor briefly. 'Come on, we'd better run for it. If we hide out in the maintenance section ...' The Doctor stopped talking, realising that Stevenson was making no attempt to move. He had drawn his blaster and was covering the door to the airlock chamber. 'Commander, come *on*,' repeated the Doctor.

Stevenson shook his head. 'Sorry, Doctor. You do what you like, but it's my job to stay here.' He turned to Lester. 'That's a fairly narrow doorspace, and we can bracket them with a crossfire from our blasters.' Lester nodded, drawing his own weapon.

The Doctor was almost tearing his hair in impatience. 'I admire your courage, Commander, but not your good sense. We're dealing with *Cybermen*. Attacking them with those hand-blasters is like hunting elephants with a peashooter. Come away while there's still time.'

But there *was* no more time. The Doctor, who had his back to the airlock door, saw Stevenson gazing over his shoulder, his eyes widening in horror. The Doctor whirled round. Towering in the doorway stood the giant silver figure of a Cyberman. Others could be seen coming through into the airlock behind it.

Stevenson could scarcely believe his eyes. He'd heard of Cybermen, even seen old pictures of them, but meeting one at close quarters like this was very different. The creature was at least seven feet tall, maybe more. It was made entirely of some kind of silvery material, that might have been either metal or plastic. There was no real difference between the Cyberman's face and body, its clothes and the many strange-shaped accessories attached to its chest.

The face was a terrifyingly blank parody of humanity, round circles for eyes, a thin slit for a mouth. Above the forehead was what looked like some kind of lamp, and two strange handle-like projections took the place of ears. There were weapons in the Cyberman's hands, plain foot-long metal rods with white cylinders on the end.

It took only a few seconds for Lester and Stevenson to get over their astonishment. 'Right, let 'em have it!' yelled the Commander.

The Doctor's cry of 'No—don't try it!' was drowned in the crackle of blasters, as both men opened fire at the Cyberleader. The silver giant reeled back a little at the double blaster impact, but showed no sign of being really harmed. It raised its Cyberweapon and the cylinder at the end glowed brightly. The Cyberleader fired, and the first shot dropped Stevenson where he stood. A second sent Lester crashing against the corridor wall and he slid slowly to the ground.

By now the Doctor was already haring along the perimeter corridor. 'Stop,' shouted the Cyberleader in its toneless inhuman voice. The Doctor ran even faster. The Cyberleader raised its weapon and fired for the third time. The Doctor spun round, crashed against a wall and dropped to the floor.

Tonelessly the Cyberleader spoke to the other Cybermen now crowding into the corridor. 'All resistance has been overcome. The Beacon is ours.' There was no triumph in its voice; Cybermen have no feelings. It was merely recording the facts.

The Cybermen spread out and began to search the Beacon, making sure there were no more pockets of resistance. One of them came to a doorway in the corridor and paused, listening. The sound of muffled banging and yelling came from the other side of the door. The Cyberman reached out a giant silver hand and tried to open the door. It was locked, so the Cyberman simply ripped it off its hinges, tearing the steel sheeting like paper. Cowering in a corner of the room was a human, and the Cyberman raised its weapon.

Terrified, Kellman yelled, 'Don't shoot, I'm your friend. I'm the one who's helping you.' The Cyberman paused. Unaware that he was using one of science-fiction's immortal clichés, Kellman said, 'Take me to your leader.'

The Cyberman said, 'Come,' and herded Kellman along the corridor. It took him to the crewroom, where the bodies of the Doctor, Lester and the Commander were piled in a heap on the floor, the Cyberleader standing over them.

It turned and said, 'You are Kellman?'

Kellman nodded, looking down at the bodies. 'You haven't killed them all?'

'Of course not. They are necessary to our plan.'

Kellman knelt by the Doctor's body and started to go through his pockets. The Cyberleader said, 'What are you doing, Kellman?'

'This is the stranger I reported, the one who calls himself the Doctor.'

The Cyberleader reacted. 'There is a traditional enemy of our people known as the Doctor.'

'You think it's the same man?'

'That is not possible. The Doctor defeated us hundreds of Earth years ago. Humans do not live so long. In addition, his appearance does not match our records. Why do you search him?'

'He was the reason I had to advance your plan. He's more intelligent than the others, more dangerous. I'd just like to know who and what he is.'

'What have you discovered?'

Kellman looked at his haul. 'So far, a bag of jelly babies, a half-eaten apple and a yo-yo. I think I'll give up.'

He got to his feet and joined the Cyberleader, who was spreading out a map on a nearby chart table. 'Is that the Vogan cave system?'

'That is correct. Once our landing is detected, the Vogans will attack us in force.'

'I shouldn't worry. They've only got light arma-
ments, nothing that will affect your Cybermen.'

'Where is the main shaft?'

Kellman jabbed a finger at the map. 'Here. I ex-
plored it for you myself. It runs deep into the very
core of Voga.'

'How far is the shaft from the transmat receptor
area?'

'A matter of yards. I set up the receptor station as
close as possible.'

The Cyberleader studied the map a moment longer.
'Excellent. You have done well, Kellman.'

The Doctor, whose system was far more resilient
than that of any human, had recovered full consciousness some time ago, and had been listening to this
conversation with keen interest. Bored with his role
of mere audience, he suddenly chimed in. 'One thing
intrigues me, Kellman, what do you get out of this—
Voga's gold?'

The Cyberleader swung round. 'There will be no
gold, human. Voga is to be totally destroyed.'

'Didn't you try that once before?' the Doctor asked
chattily.

'This time we shall not fail. You three will help us.
That is why your lives have been spared.'

'I was wondering why you hadn't killed us. But I'm
curious to know why you need our help.'

The Cyberleader pointed to the centre of the map.
'The heart of Voga is almost pure gold.'

The Doctor stood up, and strolled casually over to
the map. The Cyberman on guard at the door raised
its weapon threateningly, but the Doctor ignored the

gesture. 'Yes, I see. And gold is poison to you, isn't it?'

'Gold is inimical to our functioning,' confirmed the Cyberleader. 'Therefore three human organisms have been preserved.'

'And what are we three organisms supposed to do for you?'

'You will carry the bombs into the main shaft. Once they are all in position, they will be detonated by remote control, destroying Voga completely.'

'Killing us too, of course?' said the Doctor calmly.

'Of course. That is of no importance. You will have served your purpose.'

The Doctor looked at the grim face of Kellman, and at the impassive features of the Cybermen. Then, incredibly, he grinned.

'Well, well, well,' he said cheerily. 'Isn't it wonderful to feel wanted!'

# 7

# The Living Bombs

Captain Sheprah, the commander of Tyrum's City Militia, reported back to his chief. 'There is no further resistance in the mine galleries. The Guardians are holding a defensive position outside the Guild Chambers.'

Tyrum nodded. 'That is as I expected. Let them hold their precious Guild Hall—for the moment. Offer them a truce.'

'We could take the Guild Chambers with one determined assault.'

'And lose the lives of many of our people? No—we shall wait.'

Reluctantly Sheprah accepted the decision. 'There is one further matter, Councillor. Two humans have been captured in the galleries.'

Tyrum listened keenly as Sheprah told of the discovery of Harry and Sarah. 'It appears they were escaping from Vorus,' concluded Sheprah. 'We also captured a squad of Vorus's men. They were hunting the humans. Their instructions were to find and kill them.'

Tyrum brooded over the implications of Sheprah's story. 'Let me see the humans,' he ordered. Sheprah beckoned to a guard and despatched him to fetch Harry and Sarah. Tyrum looked grimly at his Captain. 'If Vorus has committed treason, he will be fortunate if he dies in battle before I reach him.'

'You think he is a traitor, Councillor?'

'I think he has been holding secret negotiations with the humans. Promising them gold in return for weapons.'

Sheprah, who was no politician, was baffled. 'Why should he do that? Ah, I see ...' He answered his own question. 'To seize power here on Voga!'

'Vorus has never concealed his ambition to replace me. But I never thought that even he would be reckless enough to expose us to our enemies.'

Sheprah was out of his depth again. 'You think that the humans are now our enemies? Surely they were our allies long ago?'

'After the cataclysm of our ancient past, we have survived only by regarding *all* outsiders as hostile. Now I must discover how far Vorus has involved us with these aliens.' He turned as the guard brought in the two prisoners. Sheprah left, to return to his troops.

For the second time, Harry and Sarah were brought as captives before a high-ranking Vogan. But the mild-mannered Tyrum made a far more favourable impression on them than had the blustering Vorus, though both sensed an edge of steel beneath the mildness.

Tyrum rose as they entered, and made a formal bow. 'Greetings. I am Tyrum, Chief Councillor of Voga.'

Harry was rather taken aback by the politeness of this reception, but did his best to rise to the occasion. 'Er ... how d'you do?' he stammered. 'I'm Harry Sullivan, this is my friend, Sarah Jane Smith.' Tyrum bowed again. Sarah wondered if she ought to curtsy, but decided against it, contenting herself with a short bob.

'Tell me,' said Tyrum, 'what is your mission here on Voga?' For all Tyrum's gentle manner, it was clear that he was determined to get a satisfactory answer from them.

'Mission?' said Sarah hurriedly. 'We haven't got any mission. Have we, Harry?'

'That's true enough,' Harry confirmed. 'We just came here more or less by accident. Nothing to do with us, really.'

Tyrum looked from one to the other of them. 'Explain,' he ordered.

Harry Sullivan sighed and mopped his brow. 'All right, I'll have a shot, if you insist. But I warn you, it's a very long story.'

Helped and prompted by Sarah, Harry stumbled through an edited account of their arrival on the Beacon and subsequent journey to Voga. 'And here we are,' he ended, a little lamely.

Tyrum thought over what he had heard. 'One thing confuses me. At first you spoke of this scourge that attacked the humans as a space plague. Then, later, you said that it was poison.'

Sarah shrugged. 'We're as puzzled as you are. At first everyone was convinced that it *was* an illness.'

Harry joined in. 'Then the Doctor discovered it was some kind of poison.'

Tyrum considered for a moment longer then said decisively, 'I believe your story, humans.'

Sarah sighed with relief. 'Well, it *is* the truth,' she said.

'However, if you *are* simply innocent travellers,

why did Vorus send guards after you to kill you, before you fell into my hands?' Tyrum persisted.

'I say, did he do that?' asked Harry indignantly. Tyrum explained about the captured guards and the story they had told.

'Well I'm sure I don't know why,' said Sarah, 'unless it's just pure nastiness. We haven't done him any harm.'

Tyrum was thinking aloud. 'Clearly, he feels that you are capable of harming him. He must think you know something that would incriminate him.'

'Incriminate him in what?' asked Sarah.

'Some plot against the state—and against *me*!'

'But we only met him for a few minutes—didn't we, Harry?' Harry nodded. Tyrum began to pace about the room in his agitation.

'It is something about the Beacon,' he muttered, almost to himself. 'My suspicions about Vorus harden into certainty. He has always had vast ambitions.' Tyrum turned to Harry and Sarah. 'This city in which you stand was once the underground survival chamber for our people. We have lived here ever since, those who remained of us, hidden beneath the surface of our shattered planet, unseen and safe from further attack by our enemies, the Cybermen.' There were centuries of fear and hatred in the way that Tyrum hissed this last word. He looked keenly at them. 'You have heard of the Cybermen?'

Sarah frowned. 'I've heard the Doctor speak of them. Weren't they supposed to be wiped out hundreds of years ago?'

'That reminds me,' Harry interrupted. 'The metal thing that attacked Sarah ... well, earlier the Doctor said it was called a Cybermat.' Harry could still hear the Doctor's unconscious rhyme, 'Not a rat—a Cybermat.'

There was a look of horror on Tyrum's face. 'Can it be? Has Vorus, in his madness, brought upon our heads the revenge of the Cybermen?' Tyrum made for the door. 'You will both come with me,' he ordered.

Sarah and Harry followed. 'Where to?' asked Sarah.

'To the gold mines. It is high time that Vorus explained himself!'

Vorus, at that moment, was confronting Sheprah in the area just before the Guild Hall. The two leaders had met for an arranged parley, at the heads of their respective troops.

Arrogant as ever, Vorus said, 'Well, Sheprah, what have you to say to me?'

'I offer a truce. My soldiers will hold their present positions. For the time being, we shall not attack your Guild Chambers.'

'You show good sense. Your city scum would be badly beaten.'

Sheprah controlled himself, remembering Tyrum's orders. 'We shall not attack unless we are provoked, Vorus,' he snapped. 'If we do attack, we shall sweep you aside and destroy you.' Pleased with his parting shot, Sheprah went back to his men. Vorus glowered after him, then returned to the Guild Chamber. Magrik was waiting for him. Vorus glared furiously down at the little scientist.

'Well, is the rocket prepared?'

'Another hour,' said Magrik nervously.

'We may not have an hour,' growled Vorus. 'By now the Cybermen will be on the Beacon. And we don't know how much longer Tyrum and his scum will hold off.'

'But our human agent, Kellman. Surely he too is still on the Beacon. Did we not promise to wait until he was safe on Voga?'

It was clear that Vorus was in no mood to worry about Kellman's safety. 'Circumstances have changed. It is simpler this way. Even if the Cybermen suspect Kellman's story, he will die with them before he can betray us.'

Magrik nodded. No doubt Vorus knew best, as always. 'Very well,' he said. 'I will notify you as soon as countdown is ready to begin.'

Unaware that he had just been callously abandoned by his Vogan allies, Kellman stood looking on as the Cyberleader tested the transmat beam. The blank silver mask swung round towards him. 'All is in order here. There is no malfunction at this end.'

Kellman fought to make his voice casual but convincing. 'There's a fault at the Vogan end, you see. The Doctor was unable to get his two friends back. Must be a faulty reciprocator diode. Unless you send me down to fix it, the Cybermen you send to Voga will be unable to return.'

The flat mechanical voice said, 'Your concern for humans has been replaced by concern for Cybermen, Kellman? Explain.'

Kellman felt a wave of panic. If he didn't get down to Voga in time to warn them of the Cybermen's plan, the gold he hungered for would be blown to smithereens. Worse still, he himself might be trapped on the

Beacon when the Vogan rocket struck. Unaware of each other's plans, Cybermen and Vogans were about to attempt mutual destruction—with Kellman caught in the middle. Forcing himself to speak with calm indifference, Kellman said, 'Suit yourself, but I'm only trying to help, just as I've always done. I set up the transmat on Voga, didn't I? I controlled the Cybermats for you.'

'That is true. You have been promised great rewards for your assistance.'

'And that's why I want to go down to Voga. To see that nothing goes wrong with the transmat and spoils your plans. After all, if the trouble spreads to this end, you may not even be able to get your bombs down on to the planet.'

Kellman held his breath, as the Cyberleader considered. Then to his vast relief it said tonelessly. 'Very well. But you would be wise to return as soon as possible. Once the detonation cycle commences on the bombs, it will not be arrested.'

Kellman stepped into the transmat booth, the Cyberleader operated the controls and Kellman vanished.

Marched along by his Cybermen guards, the Doctor arrived just in time to hear the end of the conversation and see Kellman dematerialise. Other guards brought Lester and the Commander along with him. Still more Cybermen were carrying objects that resembled metal rucksacks, very much like the backpacks worn by the early astronauts. The little party assembled by the transmat booth, and the Cybermen put their burdens down in a corner, handling them, the Doctor noticed, with enormous care.

The Doctor nodded towards the backpacks. 'And what have we got there then—are we going camping?'

The Cyberleader showed no reaction to the Doctor's joke. Very hard to get a laugh out of a Cyberman, thought the Doctor ruefully. But at least it gave him the information he was after. 'These are cobalt bombs. The most compact and powerful explosive devices ever invented.'

'Wasn't their use banned by the Armageddon Convention?' The Doctor was referring to a famous interplanetary treaty, in which the more intelligent races of the galaxy had attempted to outlaw some of the more lethal weapons of destruction. The Cybermen, like the Daleks, had refused to sign, or even to attend the Convention. Cybermen did not subscribe to any theory of morality when it came to war. Total destruction of the enemy was their one aim.

Taking careful note of the position of the bombs, the Doctor asked casually, 'Tell me, what inducements did you offer Kellman?'

'The matter is of no concern to you.'

'Oh, everything interests me,' said the Doctor sincerely. 'But what puzzles me is the fact that Cybermen have nothing any human could possibly want.'

'Your statement is incorrect.'

The Doctor seemed determined to be as tactless as possible. 'Well, what have you got?' he asked scornfully. 'No home planet, no position in the galaxy, no influence, nothing. You're just a pathetic collection of tin soldiers, skulking about the galaxy in a worn-out space-ship.'

The Commander and Lester looked at each other in

horror, wondering why the Doctor seemed so set on provoking their captors.

The Cyberleader took a pace closer to the Doctor, towering over him menacingly. 'You speak unwisely. The Cybermen are destined to become rulers of all the cosmos.'

'I don't think so, somehow. You tried that once, and were very nearly wiped out.'

It seemed almost possible to detect the overtones of hate in the Cyberman's voice. 'Because of Voga, and its gold. If the humans had not been able to call upon the resources of Voga, the Cyberwar would have ended in glorious triumph.'

'But it *did* end in glorious triumph,' said the Doctor infuriatingly. 'Triumph for the humans. Once they'd found your weakness, that was the end of the Cybermen.'

The silver giant took another step towards the Doctor. 'That is why Voga must be destroyed, before we begin our second campaign.'

The Doctor didn't seem impressed. 'Having another go, are you?'

The Cyberleader's voice rose in volume and intensity. 'We have parts stored in secret hiding places to build a new Cyberarmy. This time it will be invincible. Cybermen function more efficiently than animal organisms. Therefore we must rule the galaxy.'

The Doctor shook his head. 'Loose thinking, old chap,' he said, almost sympathetically. 'The trouble with you Cybermen is you've got hydraulic muscles and hydraulic brains to go with 'em.'

For some reason this childish insult finally broke through the Cyberleader's control. It took a final step forward, the silver arm sweeping upwards for a blow. As Lester yelled, 'Look out,' the silver arm swept down towards the Doctor.

The Doctor grabbed the arm, already moving backwards, converting its momentum into a series of reverse head-over-heels rolls that landed him in the corner by the silver packs containing the bombs. He grabbed one of the backpacks and jumped to his feet, holding it out before him. 'Very unstable things, these cobalt bombs,' gasped the Doctor. 'Could be very dangerous if I dropped this . . .' Deliberately, the Doctor let go of the bomb . . .

# 8

# Journey into Peril

Time seemed frozen as the bomb dropped from the Doctor's hands. Then, deftly, he caught it by one of the dangling straps. Lester and Stevenson gasped with relief, and even the Cyberleader took a sudden step backwards.

Pleased with the effect of his demonstration, the Doctor looked round. 'Now I'll tell you what you're going to do, Cyberleader. You and your crew are going back to the airlock, back into your ship, and away from here as fast as you can. If you don't I'll explode this cobalt bomb, and we'll all turn into space-dust together.'

'If you explode the bomb you will destroy yourself and your fellow humans,' droned the Cyberman.

'I know. But then we stand a good chance of being blown up anyway, so there's really nothing to lose, is there?

(From somewhere in the Cyberleader's chest-unit, an alarm signal was sending out a steady, inaudible pulse. Inaudible to human beings, that is. But in a nearby corridor the lamp in the head of a patrolling Cyberman suddenly glowed brightly, and it swung round to answer the signal.)

'Well, what's it to be?' the Doctor was asking. 'I trust you'll have the sense to live and fight another day?'

'We accept your terms,' said the Cyberleader in his

emotionless voice. Scarcely able to believe what was happening, the Commander and Lester watched as the Cyberleader and his men began moving slowly in the direction of the airlock. Still clutching the bomb, the Doctor backed away before them—and straight into the arms of a Cyberman sentry, who had loomed suddenly up behind him.

Giant silver arms crushed the breath from the Doctor's body. With a final effort he threw the bomb-pack away from him. The Cyberleader glided forward and caught it before it touched the ground, lowering it delicately into the corner with the other bombs.

The Doctor meanwhile was struggling and choking in the steely hug of the Cyberman. One massive arm was locked round his throat, cutting off the air. The Cyberleader spoke 'Do not kill him. He can still be useful to us.' The Cyberman released the Doctor, who crumpled unconscious to the ground.

As soon as he arrived on Voga, Kellman began hurrying along the mine galleries on his way to warn Vorus of the coming attack. As he ran through the gloomy tunnels, he was worried by the sound of distant blaster-fire. Something was happening on Voga, something that wasn't part of the plan.

Suddenly a powerful beam of light pinned him to the wall of the gallery. He looked round, blinking. He could see shadowy armed figures moving behind the light-beam. 'It's all right,' Kellman called, 'I'm a friend. Take me to Vorus, he's expecting me.'

Unfortunately for Kellman, he had run into a patrol of Tyrum's City Militia, who were unimpressed by the mention of Vorus's name.

'Vorus is no longer in charge here,' said the Militia Captain gruffly. 'We shall take you to see Tyrum.'

As the soldiers began to bustle him away, Kellman kicked and struggled wildly. 'No, no,' he yelled, 'you don't understand. I must see *Vorus*. I've got something to tell him. You're in danger, all of you ...' He subsided as one of the guards gave him a thump with a blaster-butt to quieten him, and he was half-dragged, half-carried away. The Militia Captain sighed. These wretched humans were popping up all over the place nowadays. Still, Tyrum would know how to deal with them.

The Doctor came round to find himself being buckled into a kind of harness by the giant hands of the Cybermen. He moved his shoulders, and felt the weight of the bomb-pack. Lester and the Commander were already strapped into their packs. The Doctor struggled to his feet, shaking his head to clear it.

'Two bombs should be sufficient to complete the destruction of Voga,' the Cyberleader was saying. 'To make completely certain, we are using three.' Cyberman hands twisted the giant metal buckles on the three backpacks carried by the humans, locking them into place.

A little shakily, but cheerful as ever, the Doctor said, 'We seem to have reached a rather interesting stage. Perhaps you could explain what's going on?'

'You would do well, all of you, to concentrate on what I am saying,' said the Cyberleader. 'Your lives depend on your understanding.' He indicated the buckles on the bomb-packs they were wearing. 'The buckles contain explosive charges, which are now primed.' He pointed to a piece of portable communications equipment, standing between two Cybermen. Its main feature was a large countdown clock, the last segment of which was coloured red. 'Any attempt to remove the harness *before* the countdown enters the red zone will cause a secondary explosion. It will not detonate the main bombs, which are now shielded, but it will destroy the human carrier and his companions. Do you understand?'

'Oh I think so,' said the Doctor. 'If we try to take off the bombs before we've put them where you want them, then we get blown to bits?'

'Correct. You would do well to hold that thought in your mind.'

'I shall,' promised the Doctor. 'Still, it doesn't really matter to us, does it? When we do place your bombs for you, we'll be blown up in the big explosion anyway.'

'Incorrect. Your journey will be timed so that you place the bombs in position just as the countdown enters the red zone.'

The Doctor looked at the clock. 'Ah, I see. At quarter to twelve, so to speak. Then what happens?'

'You will have most of the red zone period, something in excess of fourteen minutes, to make the return journey to the transmat beam and send yourself back to this Beacon. When you arrive, you will be rewarded and given your freedom.'

An old twentieth-century slang phrase popped into the Doctor's mind. 'Pull the other one, it's got bells on.' But he didn't try it on the Cybermen. Instead he asked, 'How will you know if we're obeying your instructions?'

'We shall follow your progress by radar. If you deviate from your directed route, we shall send a signal to Voga, and the relay device will explode the bombs.'

The Doctor looked at the piece of equipment crowned by the big countdown clock. 'I see. So this is the relay device, this thing with the alarm clock on? And it will be coming down to Voga with us?'

'Correct. Two guards will beam down to Voga with you, taking the relay device. They will wait by the tunnel, next to the transmat station. When you have completed your mission, you will all return to the Beacon, before the final explosion.'

'But if we stray off our route, you'll see it on your radar, the guards will beam back to the Beacon, leaving the relay, you'll press the button here, and up we go?'

'Correct. Your only hope of survival is to obey. You will leave now.'

The Doctor settled his bomb-pack more comfortably, for all the world like a hiker about to set off on a day's walk. 'Why not? I think we've covered everything.' The Doctor's mind was racing as he went over and over the plan. 'If we try to take the packs off too soon, we'll blow ourselves up,' he thought. 'If we don't go where they want us to, *they'll* blow us up. If we *do* do what they want, we'll blow up an entire planet.' The Doctor could see only one possible loophole. He could take the bombs to the detonation zone, take off the packs once the countdown clock was in the final red sector, then use his fifteen minutes not to escape, but to attempt to defuse the three cobalt bombs. It was the slimmest of chances but it was the only one he could see.

One of the Cybermen bustled the Doctor impatiently towards the transmat booth. The Doctor raised a warning hand. 'Careful, old chap! You never know, I might go off.'

The Doctor and his guard stepped into the transmat booth and were dematerialised. The two other humans, the other guard and the relay equipment were all despatched after him. The Cyberleader watched them go with satisfaction. How transparent and emotional these animal organisms were. It had been easy to follow the thoughts in the Doctor's mind. That single loophole had been left deliberately, left to give him a hope of escape, to be sure that he would follow the plan to the last. What the Doctor did not know was that his fifteen minutes' grace after removing the packs did not exist. Once the countdown clock entered the red sector, which should be just as the Doctor and his friends put the bombs in position, the bombs would explode immediately, putting an end to the Doctor, his friends and the planet Voga. The Doctor would trouble them no more. Neither would the Vogans and their gold.

The Cyberleader touched a control on the special console in front of him. The countdown had begun.

On Voga, the Doctor, Stevenson and Lester, and the two Cybermen with the relay equipment, stood by the transmat station. One of the Cybermen pointed. 'That tunnel will lead you to the main shaft, which leads to the explosion area. Here is your chart. Go.'

The Doctor took the chart and the three set off,

weighed down by their bomb-packs. On top of the relay device, the countdown clock ticked remorselessly. Beside it the two silver giants waited. Suddenly one of them alerted, pointed down the gallery. The sound of marching feet, coming nearer. The Cybermen concealed themselves in the tunnel mouth.

A squad of City Militia, on their way to join the siege of the Guild Hall, were amazed to find a piece of obviously alien equipment ticking away in one of their galleries. Breaking ranks they crowded round, examining it. One of them stretched out a hand to touch it. A Cyberman stepped from the tunnel mouth and blasted him down. A second Cyberman joined him, and the Militia broke and fled, making no attempt to return the fire. They ran along the galleries screaming with panic. The ancient nightmares had come to life. Cybermen had returned to Voga.

Trudging along the tunnel, the Doctor and his companions heard the crackle of Cyberweapons. They looked at each other but said nothing. It was easy enough to imagine what had happened. There was nothing they could do to help, and the ghastly weight of the bomb-packs on their backs was a constant reminder of their own peril.

After a moment, Lester said, 'Doctor, do you reckon they meant that stuff about giving us time to escape?'

The Doctor sighed. 'I doubt it. Once we get the bombs to the explosion zone, we'll have outlived our usefulness.'

Stevenson nodded. He too had little faith in the promises of the Cybermen. 'So what do we do, then?'

'We keep moving,' said the Doctor simply.

'Why bother?' demanded Lester. 'Why don't we just stay here?'

'Because they'll blow us up if we do—and that's a moment I'm anxious to postpone as long as possible. While there's life, you know ... Something will turn up.'

'It had better,' said Lester grimly. They all trudged on their way.

In the control-room on Nerva Beacon, the Cyberleader tracked their progress on his radar-scanner. A Cyberman approached with a message from the relay guards. 'All initial resistance has been easily crushed.'

'That is good.' The Cyberleader studied the moving dot on the radar-scope that monitored the progress of the Doctor and his two companions. 'The bomb party is now one hundred metres below the surface.'

Offering the remark as a simple statement of fact, the Cyberman said, 'Kellman has failed to return.'

'It is of no importance,' replied the Cyberleader. 'His part in the operation is now at an end.'

Kellman, by now, was standing before Tyrum, flanked by two City Militiamen. They had brought him in just as Tyrum was setting off with Sarah and Harry to see Vorus. Tyrum was subjecting Kellman to a long and patient interrogation, determined to discover exactly what had been happening on Nerva Beacon, and how it would affect the safety of his beloved Voga. Sarah and Harry stood by listening impatiently, as Tyrum went over and over the same ground. 'Tell me again,' he persisted, 'what exactly is your connection with Vorus?'

86

Kellman was in a difficult position. He did not know or trust Tyrum, knowing only that Vorus considered him an enemy. Under the circumstances, Kellman dared not reveal his knowledge of the Cybermen's plans to send living bombs to the heart of Voga. He feared this would so anger the aliens that they might execute him immediately. His only hope was to persuade Vorus to fire the rocket before the bombs could be detonated. Picking his words carefully, Kellman said, 'Vorus and I were working together. We planned to lure the Cybermen into a trap and destroy them.'

'How? What trap?'

'Nerva Beacon itself is the trap. Vorus has a rocket with an armed warhead pointed straight at the Beacon.'

Sarah looked at Harry. Neither of them was surprised to learn that Kellman had been working with the Cybermen, and also conspiring to betray the Cybermen to the Vogans. And frankly they didn't much care whether Kellman was a double or only a single traitor. But the threat to the Beacon did concern them. As far as *they* knew (thanks to Kellman's silence about the Cybermen's plan) the Doctor was still on the Beacon.

Kellman was begining to panic. 'Look, we're wasting time. While we stand here, the Cybermen are planning to blow up your planet.'

'How are they planning to do this?' demanded Tyrum.

Kellman hesitated. Perhaps he'd better tell them about the bombs after all. Perhaps their technology was sufficiently advanced to be able to disarm the cobalt bombs. He was about to speak, when Sheprah rushed into the room. 'Councillor, the Cybermen are already on Voga. They've landed on the first level.'

'How many? What are they doing?'

Sheprah was puzzled. 'According to my reports, only two. And they do nothing. They have some apparatus, and they wait, killing all who approach. Our weapons have no effect on them.'

'What about back in the Cyberwar?' interrupted Harry. 'You had weapons to defeat them then.' He vaguely remembered what the Doctor had told him about the Cyberwar.

Tyrum turned on him angrily. 'We provided only the gold. The weapons, the technology to use the gold, came from the Earthmen. That is why we were defenceless when the Cybermen attacked us.'

'You'll never stop the Cybermen,' shouted Kellman. 'Vorus's rocket is your only hope. He can blast that Beacon out of the sky.'

Tyrum came to a decision. 'Sheprah, keep guard on the Cybermen. If they attempt to move, if more come to join them, attack with every weapon we have. The rest of you, follow me We're going to speak with Vorus!'

As Tyrum and his Militiamen bustled them along the mine galleries towards the Guild Hall, one thought filled Kellman's mind. Somewhere, deep below them, three trudging figures were carrying the deadly cobalt bombs to the heart of Voga.

The Cyberleader had only to press a button, and the whole of Voga would disintegrate into a shower of flaming planetary debris. He wondered how much time they had left . . .

# Countdown on Voga

As Tyrum and his party entered the big cave that opened out before the golden doors of the Guild Hall, guards stepped from hiding, covering them with blasters. Tyrum attempted to wave them away. 'Do you not recognise me? I am Tyrum, Chief Councillor of all Voga. Stand aside!'

The Guard Captain looked dubious, but seemed prepared to listen. Tyrum was just about to demand that a messenger be sent to Vorus when Kellman, the remorselessly-ticking countdown clock of the Cybermen filling his mind, ran forward in blind panic, trying to force his way through the guards. 'Get out of the way, you fools,' he screamed. 'We've got to see Vorus, or we'll all be killed.'

Faced with sudden attack from a screaming alien shrieking threats at them, the guards' reaction was natural enough. One of them shoved Kellman brutally away, another clubbed him down with his blaster. Instinctively, Tyrum's Militiamen came to Kellman's defence, blasters were fired and a general, confused struggle broke out, with both Tyrum and the Guard Captain trying to restrain their men and sort things out.

Harry grabbed Sarah and pulled her out of harm's way; they crouched out of sight in an alcove of rocks. Sarah peeped out. No one seemed to have noticed them. She turned back to Harry. 'I'm going to try to reach the transmat. Someone's got to get back to the Beacon and warn the Doctor.'

Harry looked worried, but didn't try to stop her. He knew that Sarah had always refused to accept the role of the helpless heroine, and her mind was obviously made up. He patted her on the shoulder and said, 'All right, old girl, off you go. I'll stay here, there may be something I can do this end.'

Sarah slipped away from the fighting, going back the way they had come. Harry turned his attention back to the battle, and was just in time to see Vorus stride out through the golden doors of the Guild Hall and bellow, 'Stop! What is happening here?'

For all his faults, thought Harry, Vorus certainly had personality. The City Guards stopped firing, and the Militia did the same. Vorus spotted Tyrum and strode towards him. 'You should know better than to use force, Tyrum. Why do you break the truce?'

'Simply a misunderstanding. Vorus, our planet is being invaded. At such a time Vogans should fight together, not against each other.'

Kellman, his head bleeding from the blaster blow, staggered towards them, thrusting Tyrum aside. 'The rocket,' he gasped. 'Is it ready to fire?'

Vorus glanced at Tyrum, then decided there was no more point in deception. 'Almost. The bomb-head is now being fitted '

Kellman wiped the blood from his eyes. 'Too late! The Cybermen have already landed.'

Vorus grabbed him and shook him. 'What? If you have betrayed us, human ...'

Kellman wrenched himself free. 'I *tried* to warn you. Once they were on the Beacon they moved faster than I'd allowed for ... there was no way I could stop them.'

Tyrum pushed his way forward. 'Where is this rocket that you speak of, Vorus? It really exists?'

'Indeed it does. Come, I will show you.' Vorus was almost glad that his long-cherished Master Plan was at last out in the open.

Tyrum paused, looked round, then turned to Harry. 'Where is the human female?'

'She's gone. She's going to try to get back to the Beacon and warn the Doctor.'

Kellman looked appalled. 'She mustn't ...'

'Well, if your friend here's going to aim rocket missiles at the Beacon, of course she wants to warn the Doctor and the others. What do you expect?'

'But the Doctor's *here*,' shrieked Kellman. 'They're using him and the others to carry the bombs to the heart of the planet. The Cybermen can't do it themselves because of the way gold affects them ...' His voice choked off as Harry grabbed him.

It took Vorus and two of his strongest guards to drag Harry away from Kellman's throat. Harry was shaking with rage. 'You knew about this—and you still helped them?'

'I didn't know,' said Kellman defensively. 'Not about the plan to use humans, not at first anyway. I knew they wanted humans left alive, but I thought it was for hostages, or for interrogation. At least I came down here to warn you, I could have stayed safe on the Beacon.'

'And let your precious gold be blown to pieces,' said Harry scornfully. 'Oh no, you couldn't face that.' He pulled himself free of the guards.

Kellman mover closer to Vorus for protection. 'I didn't know about the bomb plan. I thought they'd mass on the Beacon ready to invade, and you could blow them all up.'

'And so we shall,' said Vorus confidently. 'The rocket will soon be ready.'

'Soon?' shouted Kellman. 'You fools, don't you realise what's happened? The girl knows about the rocket. If she starts blabbing to the Cybermen, they won't wait for their zero-hour. They'll explode their bombs now!'

Luckily for Sarah, the approach tunnel she emerged from took her out quite close to the Cybermen as they stood guarding their relay device. She looked at it curiously, wondering what was the purpose of the ticking clock. The single pointer was now very close to the red sector, though Sarah, of course, was still unaware of its deadly significance. She was unaware, too, that the Doctor was already on Voga. She was determined to reach the Beacon and warn him.

The transmat booth was fairly near to the guarding Cybermen, and Sarah wondered how she was going to reach it undetected. Then she heard shooting further down the tunnel. A squad of Sheprah's Militia had managed to work their way along the tunnel towards the Cybermen, and had embarked on a brave but foolhardy attack, quite against Sheprah's orders. Ignoring the blasters, the silver giants strode forward, firing as they came. The tips of their Cyberweapons glowed red, and Vogan after Vogan crumpled and fell.

Sarah seized her opportunity. She ran to the transmat booth, set the controls and transmitted herself back to the Beacon. By the time the Cybermen resumed position, their attackers driven back or destroyed, the transmat booth was empty.

As Sarah materialised on the Beacon, the Cyberleader and his second-in-command were intent upon their radar-screen, and she was able to slip unseen into hiding, behind a seemingly unused control-console in one corner. She heard the Cybermen say, 'Average progression rate is fifty metres per minute.' Sarah wondered what they could be talking about, not realising that the one doing the progressing was the Doctor.

The Cyberleader said, 'Excellent. They will reach the detonation area in seventeen minutes.'

The second Cyberman studied the radar-screen more intently. 'Distortion on our radar-scope is increasing, because of the heavy gold concentration. The three humans carrying the bombs can no longer be identified by separate signals.'

'It is not important. The Doctor does not know it. Since he believes he will still have time to escape after reaching the detonation area, he will follow our plan. He does not know that the bombs will explode when the countdown reaches the red sector.'

By now Sarah realised what was happening. She was trapped on the Beacon. And the Doctor was on Voga, carrying a bomb that was going to explode ... in seventeen minutes.

In the work-area of engineer Magrik, Harry, Tyrum and Kellman stood looking at the embodiment of Vorus's dream. His rocket, the Skystriker, towered above them. It had been built in a shaft that led direct to the planet surface, forming a kind of underground launch pad. Vorus gestured proudly towards the slim, deadly-looking rocket. 'Magrik and his team worked on this rocket for two years,' he said bitterly. 'Two years, and now we lose the race by minutes!'

Kellman grabbed his arm. 'There could still be a chance. If you can fire the rocket *before* the Cyberbombs are in position ...'

Vorus shook his head disgustedly. 'Magrik reports a delay in fitting the bomb-head. It will be another twenty minutes at least. We have gambled and lost, Kellman.'

Everyone stood looking at the rocket in gloomy, fatalistic silence. Everyone but Harry Sullivan, who had decided that it was time for some positive action. He was bitterly aware of the dilemma that faced him. If the rocket *was* fired, Sarah would die on the Beacon with the Cybermen. If it *wasn't* fired, everyone on Voga would die, himself and the Doctor included. Harry worked out the only possible course of action. The Vogans, naturally enough, would refuse to think of anything else while their planet was in danger. First, he had somehow to stop the firing of the Cyberbombs, thus saving himself, the Doctor and the planet Voga. Then, and only then, could he plead with the Vogans to delay the firing of the rocket long enough to allow Sarah to be rescued.

Harry started putting his decision into effect. He turned to Kellman, who cowered away nervously, and said, 'Is there any way, any way at all, we can stop those bombs going off?'

Kellman shook his head. 'They'll be detonated by

remote control and ... the relay! That's it. If we can destroy the relay ...' Excitedly, Kellman explained. The Cybermen's detonation signal from Nerva Beacon could only work if it was boosted by an on-planet relay device. This was the piece of apparatus the Cybermen had brought with them to Voga.

'That's it,' said Harry decisively. 'Vorus, Tyrum, you must combine your men and make an all-out attack on the Cybermen. There are only two of them, you'll have to overwhelm them by sheer numbers. Tell your troops the survival of the planet depends on it.'

'We can try,' said Tyrum. 'It is probably hopeless, but we can try.' He sent for Sheprah and gave the necessary orders. Vorus called in his Guard Captain and did the same. When the two soldiers, allies instead of enemies now, had left, Tyrum turned angrily on Vorus. 'You are insane, Vorus, do you realise that? We have both sent our men out to die—and you have brought about the destruction of your race.'

Vorus was unrepentant. 'I brought them freedom! Freedom to live on the surface, freedom from fear ... Freedom to live like Vogans, not like worms cowering in the dirt!'

Tyrum waved scornfully at Kellman. 'And this great plan was conceived in the company of such as this one. A double agent, a traitor, a murderer of his own kind ... A man whose only loyalty was to himself, and to the gold he hoped to win.'

Vorus hammered his fist on the rocket gantry. 'The plan would have worked. Just a little more time, that's all we needed ...'

Harry decided he'd heard enough speech-making.

'Look, all this recrimination is pretty pointless. There's one more thing we can try. We can get into the main shaft and somehow stop those bombs being planted. That may puzzle the Cybermen, give us a bit more time to take the relay.'

'And how do we do that?' demanded Kellman scornfully. 'The Cybermen are holding the entrance. If an army of Vogans can't get past them ...'

'Well, isn't there some other way into the shaft? This place is riddled with tunnels. There jolly well should be something we can use.'

'Only that central shaft penetrates so deep,' explained Kellman wearily. 'The other galleries simply don't connect with it.'

Tyrum intervened. 'Wait—let me think ... The shaft was widened when I was young. There was a cross-shaft, a narrow one for ventilation purposes. It *might* still be passable ...'

Harry made for the door. 'Well, for Pete's sake, let's go and see.'

Tyrum led them out of Magrik's workshop and through a maze of mine galleries. At last he paused before a dusty, hanging arras and ripped it aside. A dark, narrow opening was revealed.

'There it is,' said Tyrum delightedly. 'I am no longer young, but my memory does not play me false. I was serving as an Engineering Apprentice in those years and ...'

Harry was in no mood for reminiscences. 'Will we be able to get through it?'

Tyrum frowned. 'The passage runs for a very long way. It *should* still be passable, but it has been long-disused. The rock is loose ... it will be very dangerous.'

'That's all right,' said Harry. 'It's worth a try.'

Kellman said scornfully, 'Well, I wish you joy of it ...'

He turned to move away but Harry grabbed his arm. 'You'll do more than that, Kellman, my friend. You're coming with me.'

Kellman backed away in panic. 'No ... I won't. You're crazy ...'

Harry turned to Tyrum. 'You said yourself that this man is a traitor and a murderer. Thanks to him, your planet and my friends are in danger of being blown up. Isn't it right that he should come with me, try to undo some of the harm he has done?'

Tyrum nodded gravely. 'It is just.'

Kellman ran to Vorus. 'Please, don't let them make me. We were allies, partners ...'

Vorus pushed him away. 'The alliance is over. You failed. What do I care what becomes of you?' He turned away.

Kellman looked round at the circle of grim faces. At a nod from Tyrum, the Militiamen of his escort raised their blasters.

'Come on,' said Harry, 'what are we waiting for?'

He shoved Kellman into the dark opening, and crawled in after him.

# 10

# Explosion!

The cross-shaft was just wide enough to edge through, just high enough to move along in a semi-crouch. Jagged pieces of rock tore at their clothing, and sometimes chunks of loose rock, disturbed by their passage, crashed to the tunnel floor behind them. The air soon became filled with rock-dust and they coughed and choked as they struggled along. From time to time Kellman stopped, pleading that he couldn't go on. Harry ignored the protests, shoving him ahead ruthlessly. If there was danger at the end of the passage, Harry was quite prepared for Kellman to run into it first. He soon lost all track of time. The passage led on and on, down and down, and the journey seemed endless.

The Doctor and his two companions had very similar feelings. Their travelling conditions were somewhat better, since the shaft they were following was big enough to walk along in comparative comfort. But there was always the weight of the bomb-packs to contend with, loading down their bodies, and filling their minds with the thought of sudden death. They spoke little. Each bomb-pack bore a slave clock, which reproduced the movements of the countdown clock on Nerva Beacon. Each one of them could see the clocks on his companions' packs, could see how soon the countdown pointer would enter the red sector.

'Soon be there, Doctor,' said Lester. There was an appeal in his voice.

The Doctor gave him a cheery nod. 'Won't be long.'

'One way or the other,' grunted the Commander. He was the older of the two humans, and he was already showing signs of physical exhaustion.

The Doctor walked on. Soon he must make a decision. Should he stop now, try to get the packs off, try to defuse the bombs. Should he wait till they were in the detonation zone, and the packs could be taken off safely. Would the Cybermen give them any time? Or would the bombs explode the minute they were in place?

The Doctor looked at the slave-clock on Lester's pack, estimated times and distances, and came to a decision. In fact he did have a plan, but it was so desperate and suicidal that he had left it till the last possible moment in the hope that something safer would occur to him. Nothing had. He stopped walking, and the others stopped too. 'Time to get busy, gentlemen,' he said. 'Now let me tell you my plan ...'

Although they had no way of realising it, Kellman and Harry were moving in a line that would make their path intersect with that of the Doctor. They *were* moving—until they found the end of the tunnel blocked by a rockfall. Kellman turned in relief. 'It's blocked. We'll have to go back.'

Harry shook his head. 'Oh no. If it's blocked, we unblock it.' He squeezed to a position by Kellman and started heaving at the rock-pile. The rocks shifted—and so did other loose rocks somewhere in the tunnel roof.

'This is friable rock,' said Kellman. 'It's dangerous.

You could easily bring the whole tunnel down.'

Harry went on heaving. 'One way or another, Kellman, we're probably going to cash in our chips soon. So we might as well die trying. Now get to work.'

Reluctantly Kellman began shifting rocks. The rock pile was loose, and it was easy enough to move the boulders. In fact the ease with which the rocks moved away was alarming, as they brought others tumbling after them. Harry found a big, central boulder which seemed to be the keystone of the pile. 'Come on,' he grunted, 'If we get this one moved, we're through!' He heaved at the boulder, Kellman unwillingly helping him. The boulder stirred, came loose and shot free. Other rocks tumbled down in a growing cascade.

'Look out,' Kellman yelled his last words, 'The whole lot's coming down ...' They were surrounded by falling rocks.

The Doctor had just finished explaining his plan to Lester and the Commander when a whole section of shaft wall fell in on them, burying all three in a rumbling cascade which included rocks large and small, dirt, dust and debris, and the bodies of Kellman and Harry Sullivan as they hurtled through the air and dropped down into the main shaft. A glancing rock grazed the Doctor's head and he took a sudden and unexpected nap.

Coughing and choking, his head ringing and bruises all over him, Harry Sullivan struggled to his feet. He seemed to be surrounded by fallen rocks and fallen bodies. The nearest was Kellman, his neck twisted at a strange angle, obviously broken in the fall. Harry felt no sympathy. As far as he was concerned, Kellman had been luckier than he deserved. But next to Kellman was the body of the Doctor, slumped face down with the bomb-pack on his back. Lester and the Commander lay in a heap near by, both similarly loaded.

The pulse in the Doctor's neck was beating steadily, and Harry decided he'd soon wake up. The first thing was to get this wretched bomb away from him. Be a nice surprise when he woke up. Harry studied the complex arrangement of steel webbing and heavy buckles holding the pack in place. Surely, if he unfastened this main clip here ... Wonder the Doctor hadn't thought of that himself. As Harry reached out to touch the steel buckle a croaking voice behind him called out, 'NO! Don't touch that!'

Harry turned. Lester had struggled to his feet, face blackened with grime. He was waving desperately at Harry. 'Don't touch that ...'

'Just going to get the pack off him,' said Harry, rather hurt at this lack of welcome.

'Booby trapped,' coughed Lester. 'It'll explode.'

Hurriedly Harry snatched his fingers away. The Doctor meanwhile was stirring. He struggled over on to his back, and lay looking upwards. 'Harry,' he said gently. 'Well, if it isn't Harry Sullivan.'

'That's right, Doctor,' said Harry. 'Come to give you a hand.' He looked at the Doctor with concern. There seemed to be something odd about his manner. Maybe that knock on the head, touch of concussion perhaps. Harry gave the Doctor a reassuring smile.

'Harry,' said the Doctor, 'was it you who brought the wall of the shaft crashing down on us?'

'Well, I'm afraid it was, Doctor,' admitted Harry. 'You see, I was trying to get to you through the ventilation shaft and ...'

'And were you just about to undo my exploding pack-buckle?'

'Ah—well, you see, Doctor, I didn't know they were explosive and ...'

The Doctor struggled to a sitting position. He threw back his head and bellowed at the top of his voice, 'Harry Sullivan is an idiot!' The shout echoed round the tunnel. The Doctor got to his feet, slapped Harry on the back and said, 'Nevertheless I'm very glad to see you again. He looked across to where Lester was helping the Commander to his feet. 'Now then, gentlemen, as I was saying when we were interrupted, it's time to carry out my plan. Commander, are you fit enough to go on?'

Stevenson stretched and winced. 'I'll manage. Won't be for very much longer anyway—whatever happens.' Stevenson moved on down the shaft.

To Harry's astonishment the Doctor led the rest of them in the opposite direction. At a sharp trot, he set off back the way they had come. Stevenson continued towards the detonation area alone. The clock on his bomb-pack showed nine more minutes to zone red.


The Cyberleader had not broken his concentration on the radar-screen for a solitary second. His second-in-command approached. 'Our surface party reports constant Vogan attacks. The Vogans have been driven off with heavy casualties.'

The Cyberleader did not look up from the screen. 'Intensify the radar signal amplification.'

The Cyberman checked controls. 'It is already at maximum, leader.'

The great silver head, with its blank circles for eyes, swung round angrily. 'The signal is not satisfactory. It is impossible to interpret clearly.'

'That is due to the high gold-concentration of the planet. Gold impairs the functioning of all our technology.'

The Cyberleader knew this well enough. But his instincts told him that something was wrong. But what? 'The signal appears to indicate movement forwards and backwards. That is not possible.'

'Perhaps the humans have divided, leader. Shall we detonate now?'

The Cyberleader considered. From her hiding place, Sarah watched him, waiting in agony for his answer.

'What depths have the bomb-carriers reached?'

'Sixteen hundred metres, leader.'

The Cyberleader came to a decision. 'Then we shall wait. I estimate that they are eight minutes from the detonation zone. One bomb at least will be in place, and that will be enough. In eight minutes the accursed planet of gold will be totally destroyed.' Even in the flat, toneless voice, Sarah could detect his eager anticipation. 'The planet will be annihilated. It will be totally vaporised. Eight more minutes . . .'

At a point quite close to the tunnel entrance, but well out of sight of the two Cybermen, the Doctor, Harry and Lester were crouching down. All three were crunching up small rocks, using big ones as hammers, producing an ever-growing pile of rock-dust. Or rather gold-dust, thought Harry. The concentration of the precious metal in the soft Vogan rock was astonishingly high, and Harry estimated that the rock-dust was at least fifty per cent pure gold, and maybe more. As they worked, the Doctor suddenly asked, 'Where's Sarah?'

Harry sighed. 'I'm not too sure, Doctor. She left me to try and get back to the Beacon ...'

'What? Whatever for?'

'Well, she thought you were still up there. She wanted to warn you about this rocket.'

The Doctor struggled to remain calm. 'Er—what rocket would that be, Harry?'

Harry scratched his head. It all seemed very complicated. 'It seems the late Professor Kellman—he copped it back in that rockfall—wasn't really working for the Cybermen. At least he *was*—but he was planning to double-cross them with these other blokes ...'

'The Vogans?' prompted the Doctor.

'That's right. I'm awfully bad on names. So anyway, he lured the Cybermen on to the Beacon so they'd be a sitting target for this whacking great rocket.' Harry paused for breath. 'The only thing is, the rocket isn't ready yet, so things have gone a bit wrong.'

'Yes they have, haven't they,' agreed the Doctor. 'Just as well, if Sarah's on the Beacon.'

Lester glanced at the clock on the Doctor's bomb-pack. 'Only another five minutes, Doctor.'

The Doctor looked at the dust pile. 'How much have we got then? Oh well, it'll have to do. Harry, are you sure you've grasped all the implications of my plan?'

Harry straightened up. 'Well, it's pretty simple, isn't it? We just creep up on the Cybermen and chuck this gold-dust into their chest-units. Straightforward enough.'

Lester shook his head, and the Doctor grinned at

Harry affectionately. 'That's the idea, Harry. Well, good luck. Let's get moving.'

Tyrum and Vorus stood waiting in the workshop. The rocket was still not ready and the nerves of both Vogans were frayed. They were locked in bitter, useless argument. 'I promise you this,' Tyrum was saying, 'if our planet survives your folly, you will stand trial for treason.'

'I shall stand my trial gladly,' boasted Vorus. 'I shall tell the people my reasons, of my plan to free them ...'

The entry of Sheprah interrupted him. The soldier's face was grim and despairing. 'We are beaten, Councillor. Our people have withdrawn. So many have died that they refuse to attack the Cybermen again.'

'Order them back,' stormed Vorus. 'Command them. Unless they succeed we shall all die.'

Sheprah shook his head. 'It would be useless. They need time to regroup, to recover morale.'

'There is no time,' shouted Vorus. 'They must attack!'

Ignoring him, Tyrum put his hand on Sheprah's arm. 'Come, old friend, I will speak to them. I am no longer young ... but if I lead the last attack, perhaps they will be shamed into following me.'

The Doctor, Harry and Lester stood waiting at the head of the shaft. Peering round the corner, the Doctor could just see the two silver giants, guarding their relay apparatus. Their attention seemed concentrated away from the shaft as they looked down the tunnel, alert for further Vogan attacks. The Doctor glanced at the clock on Lester's pack. Only a couple of minutes to go ... He tapped Harry and Lester on the shoulder. 'Now!' he whispered. One by one they crept from the tunnel towards the Cybermen. Each had hands full of gold-dust.

For an amazingly long time, their luck held good. The Cybermen were concerned only with danger from the Vogans, and the thought that the humans might come back down the shaft had not occurred to them. The Doctor's party was almost within striking distance, he was poised to spring, when one of the Cybermen turned round. It was Harry Sullivan who saved them. Fresher than the Doctor and Lester, unencumbered by the heavy packs, he sprinted forward like a champion, legs pumping desperately. He moved so fast that before the Cyberman could even raise his weapon, Harry was attacking it. Since Harry was now too close to be shot at, the Cyberman caught him in its crushing steel hug, increasing the pressure remorselessly. For a moment Harry's arms were trapped by his sides, but he managed to wrench one arm free, and obeying the Doctor's instructions, he ground the gold-dust mixture into the Cyberman's chest-unit. The effect was amazing. The grip on him loosened at once and the Cyberman staggered back. Freeing his other arm, Harry applied the second dose and the Cyberman gave a weird electronic howl. It staggered back, buckled at the knees and collapsed, green fluid oozing from its joints ...

While all this was going on, the Doctor and Lester were having a much tougher time. The second Cyberman had enough warning to open fire, and they flung themselves aside just in time. Before it could fire again, they closed in, ducking under the Cyberweapon and trying to get close enough to use the gold-dust. The Cyberman drove them off with great flailing blows. First Lester, and then the Doctor were sent flying across the cave. The Doctor hit the wall, and collapsed half-stunned. The Cyberman raised its gun ...

Lester acted without thinking. He hurled himself at the Cyberman in a kind of low Rugby tackle, and sent it staggering back into the relay apparatus. As the two of them fell on top of the relay machine, Lester deliberately reached up for one of his pack-buckles ...

Harry turned from dealing with his Cyberman just in time to take in the scene. It remained for ever photographed on his memory. The Doctor slumped against the far wall, blood trickling from his temple. Lester and the Cyberman collapsed across the relay apparatus. Lester's fingers undoing his pack-buckle ...

The explosion sent Harry flying across the cave and brought down a considerable chunk of the roof. When he picked himself up he saw that Lester, the Cyberman and the relay unit were buried together under an enormous pile of boulders. Only the clock part, battered and wrenched half-off, projected from the pile. The pointer was just fractionally clear of zone red.

Harry ran to the Doctor and helped him up. The Doctor reeled a little, and recovered himself. He looked at the pile of rocks, and the shattered relay machine. Harry spoke the thought in both their minds, 'It's pretty badly smashed, Doctor, but it *could* still be working.'

The Doctor nodded. Slowly he raised his hands to his shoulders. 'I know. There's only one way to find out.' The Doctor started to unbuckle his pack ...

# 11

# Skystriker!

His fingers perfectly steady, the Doctor undid the last buckle and eased the bomb-pack from his shoulders, lowering it carefully to the ground. Harry let out a long breath. 'It's all right,' he said unbelievingly. 'It didn't go off.'

The Doctor looked at the rock pile, under which lay the shattered bodies of Lester and the Cyberman. 'Lester sacrificed himself to blow up the relay apparatus,' he said quietly. 'He knew it was the only way. With the relay smashed, the buckle-explosive charges become inoperative. The Cybermen can't detonate the cobalt bombs either.'

'So we're safe, then?'

'Only for a little while, Harry. There'll be a Beacon full of very angry Cybermen up there—they're bound to think of some other plan.'

Suddenly Harry remembered. 'And Sarah's still up there with them.' They heard the sound of running footsteps. Tyrum, Sheprah and a jubilant crowd of Vogans were coming down the tunnel towards them.

The Cyberleader stabbed angrily at his controls. 'We have lost radar contact.'

The second-in-command looked up from another row of instruments. '*All* information-flow from the planet has stopped. The countdown has ceased also.'

The Cyberleader glanced at the picture of Voga on his vision screen. 'I shall detonate by manual control —now!'

As his hand went for the detonator switch, Sarah dashed from her hiding-place and tried to pull away his arm. She was unable to move it. The other Cyberman reached out his huge silver hand, and plucked Sarah away almost casually, flinging her across the width of the control-room. She crashed into the metal wall, and slid to the floor. Ignoring her, the Cyberleader reached for the detonator switch and pulled it savagely. He fixed his eyes on the screen, waiting to see the picture of Voga disintegrate. Nothing happened. Voga hung peacefully in space, solidly and obstinately *there*. The Cyberleader crashed his metal fist down on the console. 'We have failed. Why? *Why?*'

When Sarah came to, she found herself tightly bound with some kind of plastic flex and dumped in a corner. The Cyberleader had considered killing her, but decided to keep her alive in order to interrogate her. Sarah wriggled round to a position where she could see the vision screen. Nothing had changed. The Cybermen sat studying their control console, and the picture of the planet Voga still filled the screen. Exultantly Sarah said, 'So you failed, then. Voga's still there. The Doctor's beaten you.'

The toneless mechanical voice showed no disappointment, admitted no defeat. 'We are not beaten. Our computers are assessing an alternative plan.'

'The best plan you could make is to clear off this Beacon before the Vogan's rocket . . .'

Sarah stopped, wondering if she was giving the Cybermen information that might help them.

The Cyberleader spoke harshly, 'Continue. If you do not, you will be forced.'

Sarah told herself the secret was out now anyway. 'Your friend Kellman wasn't really on your side at all,' she said with some satisfaction. 'He led you into a trap. The Vogans have a rocket aimed straight at this Beacon.'

'You are lying.'

Sarah shrugged. 'All right. Just you stick around and see, you'll find out the hard way.'

'If the Vogans had such a rocket, they would have used it before now.'

'Maybe it wasn't ready. All I know is, before I left Voga I heard Kellman urging them to use it.'

The coldly logical brain of the Cyberleader continued to evaluate the problem. 'If they have a rocket, they have not fired it. The logical conclusion is: it is not ready, or it has malfunctioned. This information does not affect our alternative plan. We shall proceed. Voga *will* be destroyed.'

In the great Guild Hall everyone was making a fuss of the Doctor, who was getting rather bored with it all.

'Human,' said Tyrum impressively, 'we shall be eternally grateful for your act in saving our planet ...'

'Please don't keep calling me "human",' said the Doctor rather peevishly. 'It's not really accurate. "Doctor" will do very nicely.'

Vorus, meanwhile, was setting the giant vision screen to show a picture of the Skystriker. 'There, Doctor,' he said proudly.

'That's your rocket is it?' said the Doctor, doing his

best to be polite. 'Yes, very nice.'

It was clear that Vorus was hurt by the Doctor's lack of enthusiasm. 'That is my Skystriker,' he said proudly. He turned eagerly as Magrik entered the room. 'Magrik, what news?'

'Everything is ready. We can begin the countdown.' Magrik looked relieved to be bringing good news for once.

'At last!' Vorus pressed a hidden button in his desk, and a panel slid back, revealing a full set of rocket firing controls. 'I have waited so long to use these . . .'

'I wonder if you'd mind waiting just a little longer?' The Doctor moved quickly across the room, and edged himself between Vorus and the controls. 'Before you do anything rash, like pressing another button, can I suggest a possible alternative solution?'

'What alternative can there be? We *must* fire the Skystriker!'

'I know how keen you are to use your little toy, old chap,' said the Doctor soothingly. 'But first, let me transmat back to the Beacon and try dealing with the Cybermen myself.'

'Yourself? You would go alone?' said Vorus in astonishment.

'All I ask is that you give me fifteen minutes. If I haven't come through on the radio to tell you all is well by the end of that time—well, light the blue touchpaper, and good luck to you.'

Tyrum came forward, putting his hand on the Doctor's arm. 'You have already done so much for us. Why should you risk your life for us again?'

'Well, it isn't really for you—it's for Sarah. She's

risked her life trying to save mine. The least I can do is to try to save her in return.' The Doctor looked at the worried faces of the two Vogan leaders. 'Just fifteen minutes,' he said persuasively. 'Is that so intolerable?'

Obviously Vorus thought it was. 'I have worked and planned for this moment for years—and now you ask me to wait.'

Tyrum spoke up, 'We owe you too much to refuse you, Doctor.'

He looked sternly at Vorus, who said, 'Fifteen minutes then—and not one second longer.'

'I'm coming too, Doctor,' said Harry firmly.

'Oh no, you're not,' answered the Doctor, even more firmly. Harry had his strong points, but secrecy and subtlety were not among them. 'Anyway, I've got a job for you. Go and find the Commander. The poor chap's still wondering if his bomb's going up or not.'

The Doctor turned to the others. 'Well, I'd better be on my way ... Oh, just one more thing. I wonder if I could trouble you for a nice big bag of gold-dust?'


Still trussed up in her corner, Sarah watched and listened as the Cyberman and his number two went over a series of complex computer print-outs. They seemed to be finalising some kind of plan. 'Point of impact?' demanded the Cyberleader.

'Twenty-three degrees, seven minutes. North one-six-zero degrees, twenty minutes East. The planetary crust is weakest at that point.'

'Velocity at impact?'

'Ten thousand light-units. The Beacon will attain

that velocity seven minutes before impact.'

'Explosive force required to disintegrate planet?'

'One thousand kilos per unit.'

The Cyberleader went over the plan in his mind once more. Nothing had been forgotten. This time failure was impossible, since no human element was involved. 'Excellent! Execute the plan. Order the necessary bomb-load to be brought to the Beacon.'

'Yes, leader.'

As his subordinate left the room, the Cyberleader turned to Sarah. 'It may be of interest to you to know our alternative plan. It is to load this Beacon with cobalt bombs, primed to detonate on impact, and then to use the Beacon's spacedrive to crash it into the planet Voga.' The Cyberleader paused to savour the horror on Sarah's face. 'At the moment of impact, we shall be observing from our space-ship. You will have a much closer view.'

The Cyberleader followed his second-in-command out of the room. Sarah began struggling desperately, hopelessly, against her bonds. Suddenly she heard the faint hum of the transmat. To her astonished delight the Doctor was beaming down at her. He hurried over, fished out a very old jack-knife and started cutting her bonds. 'Listen, Doctor,' Sarah whispered excitedly. 'The Cybermen are planning to load this Beacon with bombs and crash it into Voga.'

'Oh, dear. And meanwhile the Vogans are just itching to fire their rocket at us.' He glanced round the room and saw the Cybermat control-box Kellman had used standing forgotten on a table. 'Just bring that along, will you, Sarah, and we'll see what we can do,'

113

he said briskly, 'Quickly now!' He strode out of the room. Sarah grabbed the control-box and hurried after him.

They slipped quietly into the perimeter corridor. Cybermen could be seen coming along from the direction of the airlock. They were carrying squat black cylinders, about the size of petrol-drums. 'Fetching more cobalt bombs from their ship,' muttered the Doctor.

They heard the voice of the Cyberleader. 'Take the bombs into the impact area. Maximum urgency is imperative.'

The Doctor pulled Sarah away. 'Come on, we'll hide out in the crewroom. We should be safe enough there. Cybermen don't need to sleep!'

Magrik looked at a clock inset into the rocket control-console. 'Seven minutes to commencement of countdown,' he said. There was a pause. Suddenly Vorus snorted,

'What can the Doctor do in such a time? We should never have agreed to this delay.' His hand reached for the controls.

Sternly Tyrum said, 'Stand back from the controls, Vorus. There are, as Magrik reminds us, another seven minutes to go.'

Vorus glared angrily at him. 'Very well, Tyrum, I shall wait. But when I press this button, it will mean not only the end of the Cybermen, but a new rule for Voga. My rule.'

'That will be for the people to decide.'

Vorus waved at the Skystriker on the screen. 'This

was my idea. I planned it. I shall be hailed as the people's liberator.'

Tyrum sniffed. 'You came close to being their destroyer.'

'That will be forgotten in our triumph. The people will beg me to lead them ...'

Harry hurried in with the Commander trailing behind him. He'd found Stevenson waiting grimly for death at the end of the shaft. The Commander still looked dazed, as if he couldn't believe in his deliverance. Harry saw that old Vorus was making speeches again, and interrupted ruthlessly. 'Any word from the Doctor?'

Vorus didn't care to be cut off in full oratorical flow. 'No—nor do I think there will be ...'

'Five more minutes,' said Magrik quietly.

Vorus touched a communications switch and spoke into a concealed microphone. 'Control to firing bunker. Five minutes to countdown.'


Sarah was enjoying a welcome rest. Stretched out on a bunk, she watched the Doctor screw the base-plate back on a Cybermat.

'You really think it'll work, Doctor?' she asked doubtfully.

The Doctor looked hurt. 'Well, of course it will—I think.'

There was a hum of power, and the whole room began vibrating gently. Sarah looked round. 'What's happening?'

'They've started the Beacon's engines.'

The Cyberleader looked at the empty corner where Sarah had been thrown, and at the trailing flex on the floor. 'She has been freed. Logic suggests that the Doctor has returned from Voga. If he is on board he will attempt to thwart our plan. Search the forward areas. Locate and destroy any animal organisms.'

A Cyberman moved immediately from the control-room. The Cyberleader turned to his number two, who was at the Beacon's engine controls. 'Increase thrust ten levels.'

The Cyberman's hands moved over the controls. 'Thrust increased ten levels. Control response, normal. Engine response effective.'

'Engage hyperdrive!'

The power-hum built up steadily.

The Doctor finished final adjustments to the Cybermat's control-box. Sarah, listening at the door, heard heavy footsteps in the corridor outside. 'They're coming, Doctor. Hurry!'

The Doctor put the Cybermat carefully on the floor and pulled Sarah into an empty clothes-locker, leaving the door slightly ajar. They heard the door open, and saw a Cyberman stalk into the room. Its round eye-slots scanned the room. It began moving purposefully towards their locker. The Doctor fiddled with the control-box, and the Cybermat suddenly came to life. Its eyes glowed red, and it began moving towards the Cyberman. As the Cyberman reached out a hand for the locker door, the Cybermat sprang. It clung to the Cyberman's neck, and its twin plungers injected pure gold-dust into the Cyberman's hydraulic system. The

Cyberman gave a strange electronic screech and keeled over, just like the one Harry had killed on Voga. Sarah shuddered at the sight of the green hydraulic fluid oozing from its joints. The Doctor grabbed her hand, and pulled her out of the locker. 'Well, there's one down. Come on!' Picking up his Cybermat, rather as if it was a pet poodle, the Doctor hurried Sarah from the crew-room.

Magrik leaned forward and spoke to the firing bunker. 'Two minutes to countdown, stand by.'

Vorus could wait no longer. 'Enough of this nonsense. The countdown will take place immediately.'

Magrik looked up from his controls. 'Vorus, look. The target sensor has reacted. The Beacon must be moving!'

Vorus moved to the controls and thrust Magrik aside. 'It's moving towards us—it's on a collision course!' He snapped the internal communications switch. 'Activate the rocket. Begin countdown. I shall fire the rocket from here, when countdown is over.'

'Now just a minute,' protested Harry. 'You promised the Doctor fifteen minutes and that's what he's getting. Every last second of them.' He tried to step in front of Vorus, but the big Vogan gave him a shove that sent him staggering back. Vorus's hands were on the controls.

A voice crackled over the speaker. 'Ten, nine, eight, seven ...'

Vorus waited eagerly, hand poised over the controls. Tyrum produced a blaster from beneath his robes. 'Stand back, Vorus.'

Vorus heard only the countdown. 'Four, three, two, one . . .'

Tyrum fired. Vorus slumped forward over the controls, pressing the firing button as he fell. He twisted round to see the vision screen. The Skystriker was lifting off on a column of fire. '*My* glory,' mumbled Vorus thickly. 'My Skystriker . . .' Then he died.

The Cybermen watched on their vision screen as Voga came closer. The Cyberleader turned to his second-in-command. 'It will be a glorious spectacle. The fireball will extend one point five million miles.'

A third Cyberman entered the control-room. 'The evacuation of the Beacon is complete. One Cyber-warrior is still searching for the Doctor.'

'Recall him. If the Doctor is on board, he will perish when the Beacon strikes Voga.'

The Doctor was not only on board, but just behind them. He slipped into the control-room, put down his Cybermat and turned it loose. It sped straight for the third Cyberman, fastening on to his neck and pumping the deadly gold-dust into his veins. The Cyberman shrieked, staggering round the room in its dying convulsions. The Doctor leaped forwards, hurling his bag of gold-dust at the other two Cybermen. Unfortunately the third Cyberman stumbled right across his path and got the full impact of the second dose. It crumpled and died, leaving the Doctor facing two very live Cybermen, completely empty-handed. Since his hands *were* empty he raised them above his head. Sarah, lurking just behind him in the doorway, did the same.

The Cyberleader snatched up its weapon and took

aim. 'If you kill us now, we'll miss the big bang,' said the Doctor almost conversationally, nodding towards the vision screen. Voga was very near now.

The Cyberleader nodded slowly. 'You do well to remind me, Doctor.' He nodded to his second-in-command, who produced a reel of flex. 'You will tie up your companion, Doctor, then I shall tie you. Tie her firmly, if you wish to live a few minutes longer.'

The Doctor obeyed. On the screen the planet Voga rushed ever nearer.

'Hurry,' ordered the Cyberleader.

The Doctor looked up. 'You want me to make a good job of it, don't you?' he asked indignantly.


Tyrum looked at the control-panel clock and sighed. 'The Doctor's time is up. I fear that he has failed.'

Harry made a great effort to sound confident. 'Don't be too sure. The Doctor always leaves things to the last minute.'

The Commander looked at the vision-screen, where they could see the Skystriker rocket soaring upwards. 'Well, he's got about six minutes now, before the rocket hits the Beacon. If he doesn't transmat off by then ...'

Harry was shocked to hear how short a time was left. The Commander saw his face. 'Sorry, Harry. Now the Beacon's moving towards the rocket, same as the rocket's going towards the Beacon. Cuts down the impact time ...'

They all looked at the screen. The rocket soared higher.

The Cyberleader tested the Doctor's bonds, and then Sarah's. 'Good. We shall now return to our ship and blast clear of the Beacon. You are both very privileged. You are about to die in the biggest explosion ever to be witnessed in this solar system.'

The Cyberleader stalked away.

Sarah and the Doctor looked at each other. Then they both looked at the vision-screen, where the planet Voga seemed to be rushing swiftly towards them.

# 12

## 'The biggest bang in history'

'How long have we got, Doctor?'

'Assuming the Vogan rocket's on its way—two or three minutes. You'd better get a move on.'

'Escape, you mean? I'm afraid you made far too good a job of these knots.'

'I hope so. I tied them with a special trick sheepshank I learned from Harry Houdini. Pull your left wrist up, and your right wrist down. You'll be free in no time.'

Sarah tried it. Nothing happened. 'I'm sorry, Doctor. You must have learned it wrong.'

Magrik looked up from his instruments. 'The radar shows something moving away from the Beacon.'

'It must be the Cybership,' said Harry disgustedly. 'They're getting away.'

Tyrum shook his head sadly. 'So it is all for nothing. The rocket will strike the empty Beacon.'

'Right—except it may not be empty,' said Harry. 'If the Doctor and Sarah are still alive, they'll be on the Beacon.'

The voice on the intercom spoke. 'Engineer Magrik to the firing bay. There is a leak in the rocket fuel section.' Magrik hurried out. No one noticed him leave. All eyes were fixed on the vision-screen, where Skystriker soared ever higher.

'Well, try your right wrist up and your left wrist down. Maybe I tied it backwards.'

Sarah tried. 'The knots are moving,' she gasped. One hand came free, then the other.

'Good girl. Now, hurry and untie mine. That rocket's a bit too close for comfort.'

As soon as he was free, the Doctor made for the space-radio. 'Hullo Voga, hullo Voga, can you hear me? This is the Doctor on Nerva Beacon.'

In the Guild Hall there was wild excitement as the Doctor's voice crackled from their speaker. Harry leaned forward. 'Doctor! Are you all right?'

'Is the Commander there?'

'Here, Doctor,' Stevenson's voice came through.

'Tell Vorus the Cybermen have left the Beacon. Tell him to aim the rocket at their space-ship.'

'Vorus is dead, Doctor. No one here knows how to work the rocket controls. We could send for Magrik ...'

'No time. *You'll* have to do it, Commander. Just a second ...'

The Doctor adjusted the scanner controls. The picture on the screen changed to one of the rocket approaching. The nose-cone seemed enormous. The rocket was almost upon them.

Even as he adjusted the scanner the Doctor was summoning to his mind's eye a picture of the rocket controls on Voga. How proudly Vorus had displayed them. 'Commander, listen to me. There should be two quadrant levers on the left of the panel. Got them?'

The Commander's hands hovered over the controls. 'Got them, Doctor.'

The Doctor's voice was calm and reassuring. 'The top one controls the angle of flight, the lower is the direction and stabiliser control. Pull the top lever across the quadrant, then move the other downwards.' Trying to keep his hands from shaking, the Commander obeyed.

The Doctor and Sarah stared as if hypnotised at the screen. The rocket's bomb-laden nose cone seemed almost to touch them. Suddenly the angle of the picture changed. The head-on view of the rocket was replaced by a fleeting side view as it whizzed past them, and away into space.

The Doctor let out a long whistling breath. 'Well done, Commander. Now you've got the hang of the controls, send that rocket after the Cybership.'

'It'll be a pleasure, Doctor.'

Sarah said slowly, 'Doctor, a ghastly thought's just struck me ... We're still heading for the biggest bang in history. I mean, the Beacon is still rushing towards Voga, loaded with bombs.'

The Doctor chuckled. 'Not for long, my dear Sarah.' He switched the scanner picture back to Voga. The planet was now so near that its jagged mountainy surface seemed within reaching distance. It was rushing closer and closer. The Doctor moved over to the Beacon controls and pulled the flight-trimmer levers. They refused to budge. 'Those sneaking treacherous tin-men have locked the controls,' he yelled.

'What does that mean?'

'It means we're heading for the biggest bang in history.'

The Commander was hunched over the rocket controls, making delicate adjustments to the directional levers. Magrik was back by now, but the Commander refused to let him take over. This was one job he wanted to finish himself. Harry leaned over his shoulder. 'You're closing in, Commander. Just a touch more starboard ...'

The Commander made a fractional adjustment, and sat back. Just a few more seconds, he thought. On the vision-screen the picture now showed the Vogan rocket hurtling towards the Cybership.

The Cyberleader looked with satisfaction on his scanner. On a nearby radar-screen, no one noticed a tiny dot moving closer and closer.

Confidently the Cyberleader intoned, 'The Beacon will impact on Voga in three and a half minutes.'

Suddenly a Cyberman shouted, 'Leader, the radar-screen. A missile is approaching us ...'

The Cyberleader rapped out orders. 'Engage full thrust. Take evasive action. Deploy full energy shield ...'

He was still giving orders to deal with the situation as the Vogan rocket struck.

The Cybership disintegrated in a shattering blast of heat.

On Voga there was a stunned silence. Harry spoke first. 'Well, that's the Cybermen finished.'

'Never again will they be a threat to Voga,' said Tyrum. To himself he thought that Vorus and his rocket had come in useful after all. He would see that Vorus received full posthumous credit. A martyr was so much more satisfactory than a political rival.

Magrik looked up from the radar-screen. 'Why does the Doctor not put the Beacon back on its proper course? It appears to be still heading straight for us.'

Appalled, they all stared at the radar-screen. The Commander looked at Harry. 'He's right,' he said quietly.

Harry coughed. 'Better give him a shout, eh? He tends to have these absent-minded spells.'

The Doctor had ripped off the inspection cover of the Beacon controls, and was heaving with a heavy wrench at the massive hydraulic controls inside. They had been locked with a Cyberman's strength, and showed no signs of shifting.

'Maybe you're turning it the wrong way,' suggested Sarah. The Doctor scowled at her, and went on working. On the scanner you could almost count the pebbles on Voga's surface.

A nervous voice came over the radio. 'Er, I say, Doctor?'

Sarah went to answer it. 'Yes, Harry? The Doctor's a bit busy.'

'Hullo, Sarah. The thing is, you appear to be heading straight for us.'

'We're aware of that, Harry. Very much so. Just to cheer you up, we are also loaded with Cyberbombs.'

'And what's the Doctor doing?'

The Doctor looked up. 'I'm doing my best, Harry,' he yelled. He gave a final heave, the massive locking nut gave a little, and then came free. The Doctor flung down the wrench with a clang and ran back to the controls. They could hear the engines roaring now as they entered Voga's atmosphere ...

In the Guild Hall, the picture of the approaching Beacon completely filled the giant vision-screen. Tyrum fell back screaming in panic. 'It's going to hit! It's going to hit!'

The Doctor leaned over the Beacon controls. 'That should do it. Now, if only she'll answer in time ...' He heaved on the flight trimmers. This time they moved freely. Sarah saw the close-up of Voga on the screen tilt and move away from them. She clutched at the console for support as the floor rocked under her. As the Doctor wrestled with the controls, the surface of Voga zoomed closer and then lurched away again. The peak of what looked like a small mountain rushed straight towards them.

Sarah screamed, 'We're going to crash, Doctor.'

'Hang on,' he yelled encouragingly. 'Can't pull back too sharply at this speed or the Beacon will break up. Wasn't built for acrobatics, poor old girl.' He eased the levers back ...

Miraculously the mountain vanished from the screen to be replaced by empty sky. The Doctor made a few more adjustments, and locked the controls. He stepped back, shaking his head, almost unable to believe that they'd survived. 'I've put her on automatic. She'll return to her proper orbit now.'

He saw that Sarah was staring over his shoulder, her mouth wide open. In an uncanny silence, the TARDIS was materialising on the other side of the control-room. The Doctor gave a satisfied nod. 'Splendid timing. I'd better just set the drift compensators. Don't want her wandering off again.' Fishing out his key, the Doctor entered the TARDIS.

There was a faint hum from the transmat booth and Harry materialised, shaken but cheerful. He stepped out, and looked towards the TARDIS. 'I see old faithful's turned up again?'

Sarah nodded, surprised to find herself as calm as he was. She supposed so much had happened recently that they'd both lost the capacity to be surprised. 'It's all go, isn't it?'

The Doctor popped his head out of the TARDIS. 'Ah, there you are, Harry. Don't just stand there, you two, come on inside.'

As they entered the TARDIS, Harry was protesting, 'The Commander will be up in a minute. Old Tyrum too, probably. Shouldn't we wait and say goodbye?'

The Doctor operated the door controls, and started take-off procedure. 'Better not, Harry. Simpler to slip away. Besides, I'm wanted urgently back on Earth.'

'How do you know that?'

The Doctor pointed to an odd-looking technical device, bleeping away in a corner. 'Because I left the Brigadier a Space-Time telegraph, for use in case of a real emergency.'

The familiar groaning noise filled the TARDIS as she took off. Raising her voice, Sarah said, 'And he's used it—this telegraph thing?'

'He has.' Take-off noise died away. The TARDIS was in the Space-Time vortex once again.

Harry gave the Doctor a sceptical look. 'Are you

really sure that bleeping is the Brigadier calling us from Earth?'

'Of course I am, Harry.'

Sarah could understand Harry's feelings. The Brigadier, their old friends in UNIT, and twentieth-century Earth seemed like an infinitely remote dream. Were they really going back this time?

The Doctor seemed to sense their disbelief. 'Now see here, you two. I can even tell you exactly where on your little planet the Brigadier's calling from. To the nearest mile or so!'

Harry and Sarah just looked at him.

The Doctor crossed over to his telegraph device and touched a control. A miniature screen popped up. It showed a picture of the Earth. The Doctor made adjustments and the picture narrowed down to show Europe, then the British Isles, then Scotland, then a particular part of Scotland. The Doctor peered at the screen, his face alive with excitement. 'I say, this is interesting,' he cried. 'I wonder why the Brigadier's calling us from somewhere near Loch Ness?'*

* You can discover the answer in 'Doctor Who and the Loch Ness Monster'.